MW00532037

CONTENTS

Case of the
Fleet-Footed Mummy

Corgi Case Files, Book 2

J.M. Poole

Sign up for Jeffrey's newsletter on his website to get all the latest corgi news-- www.AuthorJMPoole.com

Case of the Fleet-Footed Mummy
Published by Secret Staircase Books, an imprint of
Columbine Publishing Group, LLC
PO Box 416, Angel Fire, NM 87710

Book layout and design by Secret Staircase Books
Cover images by Yevgen Kachavin, Erik Lam, Felipe de Barros

First Secret Staircase paperback edition: November 2020
First Secret Staircase e-book edition: November 2020

* * *

Publisher's Cataloging-in-Publication Data

Poole, J.M.
Case of the Fleet-Footed Mummy / by J.M. Poole.
p. cm.
ISBN 978-1649140210 (paperback)
ISBN 978-1649140227 (e-book)

1. Zachary Anderson (Fictitious character)--Fiction. 2.
Pomme Valley, Oregon (fictitious location)—Fiction. 3. Amateur
sleuth—Fiction. 4. Pet detectives—Fiction. I. Title

Corgi Case Files Mystery Series : Book 2.
Poole, J.M., Corgi Case Files mysteries.

BISAC : FICTION / Mystery & Detective.
813/.54

To Giliane —

I don't think I can say it enough times in one day. Thank you for all that you do. You've helped me out in more ways than you can possibly imagine. Love you always & forever!

ACKNOWLEDGMENTS

I have several people to thank when it comes to publishing this book. Of course, I have to thank Giliane, my wife. Once more she worked closely with me to make sure I didn't screw anything up in our fictional town. I also drew on her experiences with "Apple Hill", a festival much like "Cider Fest", located in Placerville, CA. If you happen to be in the area when it's open then I would definitely recommend you check it out!

I'd also like to thank the members of my Posse. They sacrifice their time in order to help me make sure the book is as polished as I can get it. You guys & gals know who you are. ☺

The cover illustration was done by a talented artist by the name of Felipe de Barros, from DeviantArt.com. It was his first time making a cover for me and I have to say that he hit it out of the park. Thank you so much, Felipe! The typography, if you can believe it, was done by yours truly. I think I'm getting better at it. I would like to point out that the 'mummy' effect on "Fleet-Footed Mummy" was provided by an artist by the name of Sonarpos. If you like to dabble with Photoshop and all the many things it can do, I encourage you to check out his work.

And — as always — I'd like to acknowledge you, the reader. Thank you for encouraging me to do what I enjoy doing most: writing. Happy reading!

J.

ONE

So how bad is it?"

The bearded man in the pressed white coat nervously cleared his throat. He removed the stethoscopic earpieces from his ears and regarded the patient with an unreadable expression. I literally felt my blood run cold. My skin broke out in goose bumps as a chill trickled down my spine. I got the distinct impression that the doctor was uncertain how to best phrase his answer. I vowed to whatever deities that existed if bad news came out of his mouth then I was gonna personally punch Harry in his. Lucky for me, they were both one and the same person.

"I don't know what to tell you, man," Dr. Harrison Watt admitted.

He looked at me and gave an apologetic smile. He may be my best friend in town, and we may have been friends since high school, but I was ready to smack that smile right off his face. I scowled and tried to look as intimidating as possible.

"You have to do better than that, pal," I crossly

told him, as I looked down at the small table in the examination room. "You need to tell me what's wrong. I swear, if you've given me a dog with a terminal disease then I am personally going to drop kick you into next week."

We both looked down at the patient. Two soft, doleful eyes looked up into mine. My stomach sank. I wasn't going to let anything happen to one of my dogs. I couldn't. I'd spend every last cent in the bank if I had to, which—and I am still getting used to this—is considerable. I couldn't let anything happen to her. I wouldn't.

Harry laid a hand on my shoulder.

"Zack, what we have here is … how do I put this?"

"Just spit it out, pal," I snapped, growing angrier and more scared by the second. "Just tell me what's wrong with her, okay?"

"Your dog is suffering from gastrointestinal distress. That is what's causing her to flatulate."

"Gasintestro what?" I repeated. Medical doctors and their big words. Whatever that was didn't sound good at all. "And it's causing her to do what?"

"Gastrointestinal distress," Harry carefully repeated. "It means Watson has gas."

A smile formed on my friend's face as he gently stroked the patient's fur. I stared at Harry, waiting for a punch line I was certain was forthcoming. When my friend didn't volunteer anything else I scowled again.

"You're telling me she has gas? And stop rolling your eyes every time you say her name. Her name is Watson. End of story."

"Watson is not a proper name for a little girl. I don't care what you say, she doesn't deserve to be called that."

"Let's forget about her name for a moment," I sputtered, jumping back to the bigger problem. "You said she has gas? It's not fatal, is it?"

Harry's smile grew even bigger.

"No, it's not fatal, Zack."

"Well, um, what causes it? Dude, they're raunchy!. Every time she lets one rip, I swear my eyes are gonna melt in their sockets."

Harry's smile quickly melted into a frown.

"Do you actually hear her pass gas?"

I shook my head. "No. You can't hear them, pal. They're silent bombs."

Harry leaned back against the counter on the opposite wall, draped his stethoscope around his neck, and stroked his chin. I'm sure I cocked my head like an inquisitive dog as I stared at my friend. I've never seen him look so pensive and serious. It was very unbecoming on him and, I will admit, a little unsettling.

"What have you been feeding her?" he finally asked.

"Only the kibble you recommended," I answered.

"No table scraps?"

"None."

"Hmm. How does she eat?"

"Excuse me? How does she eat? What kind of a question is that? She doesn't use a fork and knife, if that's what you're asking."

Harry cracked a smile and shook his head.

"No, what I mean is, the cause of most cases of flatulence in dogs comes from swallowing air."

"Why in the world would dogs willingly swallow air?" I asked, perplexed.

"Brachycephalic breeds, for example, are prone to swallowing extra air due to their short necks and the position of their noses."

"Brachy..."

"Brachycephalic," Harry slowly repeated.

I looked down at Watson just as she turned to look up at me.

"Are corgis braky ... brachy ... whatever you just said?"

"No."

"No? Dude, why'd you bring it up?"

"I was giving you examples. You asked why a dog would swallow air. I was giving you an answer."

"Well, what kind of dogs are?"

"Are what?" Harry mischievously asked, clasping his hands behind his back.

"You know good and well what I mean. I'm not saying that word again."

"You haven't been able to say it yet," Harry pointed out.

I crossed my arms over my chest and glared

at Harry. This was a side of my friend that I did not like. The pompous jerk was showing me up, proving he had more education than I did. Harry laughed and slapped me on the back.

"Pugs. Bulldogs. Boston terriers. Pekingese. Are those enough examples for you?"

"So if Watson—"

"Pumpkin," Harry interrupted, squeezing the word in between coughs. He had made no qualms about telling me what name he would have given my newest dog.

"If Watson," I continued, glaring at Harry, "isn't one of those breeds, then what's causing the gas? Come on, Harry. She farts in my Jeep. She farts in Jillian's store. She even farts when she's up on the bed with Sherlock and me. There's gotta be a reason why."

Harry was doubled over with laughter.

"You're not helping," I told him crossly.

"Look," Harry said, trying valiantly to compose himself, "the reason I asked you how she eats is because the most likely reason, like I said, is that she's swallowing air. She probably doesn't even know she's doing it. So, how does she eat? Does she gobble her food up the moment you put it in front of her?"

I had opened my mouth for an angry retort when I thought better of it. I thought back to all the feedings I had given my dogs. Sherlock was slow and methodical when it came to eating, selecting each piece of kibble as though he was the world's foremost food critic. Watson, on the other hand, was a canine vacuum cleaner. She was always done in less than twenty seconds. I timed it once. The fastest I've seen her polish off her kibble was a record breaking eleven seconds. Was that the source of her gas? Was she simply eating too fast?

"Okay, if that's her problem, how do I make her stop?"

Harry shrugged. "Get her a different bowl."

"Huh?"

"They have special dog food bowls specifically designed to make it difficult for the dog to eat. They have these designs built in to the bowl, making it challenging for the dog to get to the kibble."

I frowned. "Designs? Like what? Can you give me an example?'

Harry made a spinning motion with his finger.

"I've seen bowls that have a swirl in it with high ridges. The kibble falls into the ridges and forces the dog to work at it in order to get the kibble out. Therefore, it slows them down."

"That sounds cruel. I don't know if I could do that to Watson when all she wants to do is eat."

"It's perfectly safe, Zack. It won't hurt her. It'll just slow her down."

"I just wish I knew why she was eating so fast." I let out a sigh. "I still can't get used to seeing you in that white coat."

Harry grinned. "There are times when I can't believe it, either. As I was saying, the only thing I can think of is that Pumpkin's previous owners..."

"Watson," I hastily corrected.

"...might have had other dogs and Pumpkin, er, Watson felt like the only way she'd be able to eat was if she literally inhaled her food as fast as she could."

I wrapped a protective arm around Watson, who, in turn, licked my hand.

"That sucks. The poor thing must have gone through hell. How can people be so thoughtless? I'd never do that to either Sherlock or Watson."

Harry raised both hands as if he was being held at gunpoint.

"Hey, we don't know for certain that's what happened to her. I mention it only as a possibility."

"So that's the only way to get her to stop eating so fast? Give her the food bowl from hell? If she's already been traumatized with eating, then the last thing I want to do is to make it even more difficult for her. There's gotta be another way. Seriously, man, her farts smell like rotten broccoli."

Harry's grin was back.

"Sherlock doesn't try to eat any of her food, does he?"

"No."

"Then, if you truly don't want to try the special dog bowl, my only suggestion would be to give it some time. Maybe she'll snap out of this behavior once she realizes there are no perceived threats."

"And if she doesn't?" I asked.

"Then you're going to have to get used to having a farting dog on your hands. Just have a can of air freshener handy and you'll be fine."

"That's just peachy," I moaned.

Watson turned to gaze adoringly up into my eyes. I ruffled her fur and set her back on the ground. The red and white corgi shook herself for a few moments and then trotted to the closed door. Clearly, she was ready to go home.

"Keep her on that diet," Harry instructed, "and make sure she doesn't get any scraps. No human food. She's a dog, remember that."

"I've never given either of them any people food," I pointed out. "And I don't have any plans to start."

"I know you haven't. I can tell just by looking at her. I'm just saying that you're doing the right thing. Don't cave, no matter how much she begs."

My cell phone started ringing, filling the lobby with the dulcet tones of Twisted Sister, singing We're not gonna take it. I fumbled with the phone for a few seconds—nearly dropping it—before I was finally able to silence the blasted thing. It was my turn to offer a sheepish smile.

"Sorry. Forgot to switch the stupid thing to silent mode before I came in here."

"Awesome choice of tones there, bro," Harry told me as he handed the clipboard to one of the girls manning the front desk. He leaned over the counter to look at my phone. "Anyone I know?"

"It's Vance. I can call him back."

"We're done here," Harry told me. "Just take the call."

"Fine." I tapped a finger on the cell's display. "Hey, Vance. What's going on?"

"Zack. Did I catch you at a bad time?"

I held my credit card questioningly up to Harry, who shook his no. I nodded in appreciation and turned to leave.

"No. Watson and I were just leaving Harry's office."

"Oh? Is everything alright?"

"Yeah, thanks for asking. Harry was just checking Watson out to make sure she's okay."

"I still say that's a strange name for a female dog."

"I've already heard the same thing from Harry today. Don't you start up either."

"Tell me again why you named your dog Watson?

"It went with Sherlock, okay?"

"But she's a girl! Watson is a boy's name."

"It was my decision. I like how Sherlock and Watson sound together. She doesn't have a problem with it so I fail to see why you should, either."

"I thought you told me last week that you now consider yourself a dog lover. Why put the poor girl through that?"

"Fine. I'll admit I thought it'd be cute. Besides, I've been through this with Jillian, with Harry, with you, and a slew of other people. She likes it, she responds to it, end of story. Is that why you called? To give me grief about my dog's name?"

I heard Vance laugh.

"Hardly. You asked for my help with a personal problem, remember?"

Vance was—is—a detective for the Pomme Valley Police Department. We met a few months ago when I had the unpleasant experience of sitting on the wrong side of an interrogation table. Accused of murder. However, that's a story I've already told and I don't need to go back down that road right now.

Anyway, I had been getting harassing phone calls in the middle of the night. There was never anyone there. I could never hear anyone say anything. The only thing I could hear was someone breathing softly into the phone. The logical assumption was that a distant member of my late wife's family was the culprit. Long story short, Bonnie Davies, the person that I had inherited my house from—and my winery—had bequeathed everything to my wife and me. Since Samantha died in a car accident last year that meant I was the lone beneficiary.

It's certainly a fantastic way to make new friends, believe you me. Man alive, had that pissed some people off. High on the list was Abigail Lawson, Bonnie's daughter. I can only assume she was doing everything in her power to make my life miserable, hoping I'll throw in the towel and just move away.

Well, it ain't gonna happen, lady. PV is my

home now. You'd better get used to it.

So, since the calls kept coming, I had enlisted the help of my detective friend. Hopefully, he had some insight into what I could do to get these people to leave me alone. I was tired of being woken up at 3:30 a.m. every single morning, almost like clockwork.

"So what do you have for me?" I optimistically asked.

"The calls are being made from a disposable phone. There is no way to track that. I'm sorry, but there's nothing we can do."

"Swell."

"I do have a recommendation."

"I'm listening."

"How often do you use the landline? Just get rid of it. That's what I did. I've always got my cell on me so I never miss a call."

"If that's my only option, then I'm willing to entertain it. Abigail can suck it for all I care."

"You don't know if Abigail is behind this."

"You have to admit, she's a fine suspect."

"You do have a point. Hey, have you talked to Jillian today?"

"No, why?"

"Do you have plans for the night?"

I reached my Jeep, loaded Watson into the passenger side, and nudged Sherlock—curled up in the back seat—to wake him up. I had to think for a moment. Did I? I shook my head, forgetting that Vance wasn't able to see me. I had yet to talk to

Jillian today. In fact, for the past hour or so, I had been trying to come up with an excuse to stop by her store. As far as plans go, Watson's checkup was the only thing I had on my calendar. That and to finish the draft of my latest book.

"Why? What's up? What do you know that I don't?"

"I thought you might like to swing by the school and see the Egyptology exhibit. The grand opening is tonight. It opens to the general public tomorrow. Tori has VIP passes."

Tori is Vance's wife; in case I hadn't mentioned anything about her before. She is a tall, lithe woman with long red hair and sparkling green eyes. Wickedly smart. She can make both Vance and me feel like grammar school dropouts whenever we're in the same room together. Jillian, however, is another story. I think she could give Tori a run for her money.

"We're talking about the high school, Vance. I read in the paper that the exhibit is being set up in the school auditorium. It's not like it's a rock concert. I can't imagine what a VIP pass to that exhibit would do for us."

"Tori says that it'd be well worth our while to check it out. Come on, man. Don't make me suffer through that by myself."

"Ah. There's the real reason. Look, I wouldn't mind going, but I don't have anyone to watch the dogs."

"Couldn't you just crate them for a few hours?"

"Crate them? Are you out of your mind? No way. Would you do that to Anubis?"

Anubis was Vance's German Shepherd. Gorgeous dog, if a touch intimidating. That dog's eyes could drill holes right through you.

"Sure. I've done it before."

"Let me rephrase that. Would Tori ever do that?"

Perhaps I should have clarified. Anubis was Tori's dog. Vance's wife was a born again dog lover and there was no way she'd ever crate her precious dog.

"Er, no."

"Didn't think so. Is this important? I might be able to get Jillian to watch them for me."

"That's not gonna work, buddy."

"Why not?" I asked, growing confused.

"Because she's accompanying you tonight."

"She is?" I asked, dumbfounded. "Since when? And how would you know?"

"Tori and Jillian are good friends. Besides, I overheard Jillian say she'd never pass up a chance to go to a formal event."

"Wait, what? Formal? To a high school auditorium?"

"That's right, pal. The tuxedo shop closes at 3 pm. Better get going."

I stared at my phone in shock and horror. A tuxedo? Me? I hated them. With a passion. The last thing I wanted to do was to get trussed up like a penguin and bump elbows with similarly dressed

JEFFREY POOLE

penguins.

"Look, Vance. Maybe this isn't for me. I'm not a big fan of dressing up. Besides, if I'm escorting Jillian to this shindig, then I don't have anyone to watch the dogs."

"Just bring them over to my house," Vance instructed. "My kids can watch them. Besides, Anubis, Sherlock, and..."

"Her name is Watson, pal," I hastily interrupted.

"I was gonna call her Watson. Take it down a notch. Anyway, all three dogs get along great. Drop them off here and we can all head to the school together."

"You owe me for this."

"Oh, just relax. It'll be a night you won't soon forget."

Well, I had to hand it to Vance. He wasn't wrong. In fact, in less than two hours, the exhibit we were heading to would be the talk of the town for months to come.

* * *

"I don't know about this," I grumbled as I yet again tried to loosen the hangman's noose around my neck.

Grr ... bowties. I should have just gone with my gut instinct and chosen the clip-on rather than the real thing. Jillian had assured me that not only would it look better, but the people at these types of events could spot a clip-on from a mile away.

I was told these type of people had a bad habit of looking down their noses at anything even remotely less than the best.

Let's set the record straight on something. I personally don't give a rat's ass what anyone thinks about me or how I look, and have said as much to Jillian on more than one occasion. However, as was typical in these types of circumstances, her argument-cancelling smile had won me over. I have never cared—or wanted—to bump elbows with the city's upper class and, I'm sure my defiant behavior was written all over my face. With extreme reluctance, I agreed to spend the evening in a form-constricting tuxedo.

Dammit.

"Stop that," Jillian scolded as she batted away my hands after I tried yet again to ditch the feeling I was being throttled. "You're going to mess it up. Trust me, you look very handsome."

I glanced over at my date for the night. Jillian Cooper owned and operated Cookbook Nook, a specialty cookbook store located downtown. She was in her mid-thirties, had long curly auburn hair, green eyes, and—like me—didn't have any tattoos or extra piercings. She kept herself fit by the simple fact that she was always on the go, a prerequisite, I'm told, of running your own business.

Jillian looked absolutely amazing. She was wearing a purple chiffon evening dress with half sheer sleeves, which had a net overlay with corded lace giving the sleeves and neckline a scalloped appearance. The chiffon skirt draped to the ground in a floor length sheath style. Her hair was done up in what she later told me was referred to as a 'side shaped coif.' I couldn't quite tell what she had to do to get her hair to look like that, but I knew one thing: she looked absolutely stunning. I scratched at the bowtie encircling my neck. Jillian promptly swatted my hand away.

"Sorry. Force of habit. It feels like I'm being strangled."

"Oh, stop your fussing. How often do you get dressed up like this? Try and enjoy the evening. Don't forget those things are harder to tie than they look. I had to tie yours, remember?"

I gave my bow tie a last, furtive scratch.

"Hey, as long as I'm standing next to you then I won't have to worry about a thing. Everyone will be looking at you, not me."

Jillian inserted her left arm into my right.

"Oh, that's so sweet! Thank you."

We followed Vance and Tori into the crowded auditorium. Spotlights and track lighting were everywhere. Stanchions and soft red velvet ropes guided us to the center of the huge space. Large tables had been erected and covered with thick black velvet. Sparkling clear glass display cases were situated on several of the tables. Glittering jewels beckoned enticingly in their respective cases and attracted small admiring crowds.

I sighed. Jillian was right. I was glad that I came

to this. A small part of me had wanted to just blow the evening off, but thankfully I managed to talk myself out of it. Egyptology exhibits were something I typically avoided due to the strong likelihood that I'd encounter that which creeped the bejeezus out of me.

More on that later.

"This is nice," Jillian whispered in my ear. "Listen! Can you hear that?"

Unsure of what I should be listening for, I paused. I heard the soft murmur of several dozen conversations. I heard the clink of champagne flutes as people drank to a variety of toasts. Someone coughed nearby. I looked at Jillian and shrugged.

"What am I listening for?"

"The music. Tori was right. It's exquisite!"

"The music?" I closed my eyes and tried to will away the ambient noise. There, barely perceptible above the din of the hundreds of people at the exhibit, were the dulcet tones of flutes and harps.

"Okay, now I hear it. Sounds like elevator music. What about it?"

Jillian playfully swatted my arm.

"You uncultured barbarian. What you're listening to is an arrangement especially written in the Phrygian dominant scale of medieval Egypt. Isn't that fascinating?"

Both of my eyebrows shot up.

"And you knew this off the top of your head? That's impressive."

"Well, no," Jillian admitted. "I didn't. Not at first. Tori told me about it. One of the curators specializes in ancient music and wrote the piece specifically for this tour."

"I wonder what they've got behind the curtain," I mused, turning my attention to the stage located at the front of the auditorium.

"It's a stage," Jillian pointed out. "Stages have curtains. They've got a podium up there. I'd say that's where the presenter will address the crowds."

I pointed at the four different spotlights illuminating the entire stage, from left to right.

"They wouldn't have that many lights trained on the stage if they weren't planning on doing something."

"That's where the big reveal is going to happen!" a woman's voice said behind me.

I turned at the sound of the voice. Tori was back and she was standing next to her husband. Each of them were holding two champagne flutes. Tori handed her extra flute to Jillian while Vance handed his to me.

"I'm so glad you two could come with us tonight!" Tori exclaimed. "I've worked so hard to get Exhibitions to come here. Now that it's finally happening I don't know what I'm going to do with my free time."

"Maybe now you'll be able to relax," Vance gently teased. "You've been so stressed these last couple of weeks."

I watched Tori level a neutral stare at her husband. "You try juggling two jobs and organizing a petition to get Egyptian Exhibitions to stop by a small town like PV for a week. I'm honestly surprised I was able to pull it off."

"Maybe it was because you petitioned them daily for three months straight," Vance idly suggested as he lifted the glass to his lips.

I stifled a smile as I watched Tori frown at Vance. The detective smiled sheepishly and pretended his champagne had become the most important thing in the world. I looked back at Tori and cleared my throat.

"Did you say you were working multiple jobs?" I asked. I knew she was a school teacher but didn't know anything else about her.

Tori nodded. "That's right. I teach here at the high school. History. I also teach dance three nights a week down at the rec center next to City Hall."

"She's the best jazz dancer in PV," Jillian proudly announced, drawing a small smile of appreciation from Tori. "She's also one heck of a traditional Irish dancer. I'm still hoping you'll start teaching one of those classes, Tori. I'd love to give it a try."

Surprised, I turned to Tori and nodded appreciatively.

"Irish dancing? That's impressive. Is that the dance where all the dancers hold their arms motionless at their sides? I've seen some of the videos. How those dancers can move like that is beyond me."

Tori smiled at me. "If I were to start a class on Irish dancing, would you and Jillian be my first students?"

Oh shit on a stick. I walked right into that one.

"Umm..."

Jillian looked expectantly up into my eyes. I usually can't tell when I'm blushing but right then I could. Suddenly it felt as if I had walked under a heat lamp. I caught Vance smirking at me.

"Why, that would a great idea," Jillian exclaimed as she tightened her grip on my arm. "What do you say, Zack?"

It was time to wipe that smug smile off of Vance's face. If I was going down, then I was taking someone with me. If I was going to suffer through one of these dance classes then so was he because, no matter how I tried, I couldn't imagine my friend, the detective, trying to learn to tap dance. Well, if you want me to be honest, I couldn't imagine myself doing that, either.

Jillian flashed me another smile. Unbelievable. What we gullible men will do when a pretty girl bats her eyes continues to blow me away.

"Fine. Tell you what. We'll sign up..."

Jillian squealed excitedly. Clearly she didn't think I'd go along with this.

"...if Vance takes the class with us."

The smile disappeared from Vance's face in the blink of an eye.

"Really? You had to drag me into this?"

"Misery loves company, pal."

"Oh, hush," Jillian scolded. "You're not going to be miserable. In fact, I think you'll love it! I've always wanted to learn how to tap. What about you?"

"I can honestly tell you that it has never crossed my mind," I confessed, patting Jillian's hand. "Not even once."

Tori laughed. "Okay, you guys. It's not going to happen any time soon, so relax."

Vance and I started to smile.

"But it will," Tori continued. "Mark my words. I will look forward to seeing you three in tap shoes."

Our smiles vanished as quickly as they had appeared. Tori hooked her arm through Vance's and led the grumbling detective off. I looked over at Jillian and shook my head. She owed me big. Me? Taking a tap dancing class? It was official. Hell hath frozen over. Words could not adequately describe the size of the favor Jillian now owed me. So, the question was, how should I collect?

"A penny for your thoughts?" Jillian asked.

"I'm trying to figure out what favor I can ask that will be in the same ballpark as the one I just did for you."

Jillian giggled, "Very well. Fair's fair. Ask away. However, once you discover that you enjoy Irish dancing then the favor becomes null and void or else you'll owe me a favor. Do we have a deal?"

"Absolutely. There's no way that I'm going to enjoy tap dancing."

Jillian smiled cryptically at me and pulled me toward a small group of people chatting amiably amongst themselves.

"I can't wait to hear you admit that you were wrong."

"Nice try, lady. Ain't gonna happen."

"Mm-hmm. Would you like to meet some friends of mine?"

"More friends of yours? Sure. Is there anyone you don't know?"

"Not really. I pretty much know everyone in Pomme Valley."

"Not surprising," I added with a smile. "You've mentioned before that you have been living here your entire life."

Jillian nodded. "True. Have you met any of them before? No? Hmm. Perhaps I should give you a little background before we make it over there."

Well, color me intrigued.

"Oh? Alrighty then. My curiosity has been piqued. Who do we have over there?"

"Do you see the lady on the far left?"

"The one with the straight long brown hair?"

"That's right. That's Hannah Bloom. She owns The Apple Blossom. Its PV's one and only flower boutique. She's married to an emotionally abusive husband. She doesn't spend a lot of time at home. She and Colin practically live in her store, so obviously don't say anything."

"Colin?"

"Oh. Sorry. He's Hannah's ten-year-old son."

"Ah. It is sad that her husband treats her like that. No one should have to live like that."

"Her husband is a douchebag," Jillian agreed, causing me to snort with surprise. "I've been trying to get her to leave him for years but she just won't do it. It's heart-breaking."

"Got it. Who's on her left? The one with the short blonde hair and all the piercings? Looks like she has at least ten earrings in each ear."

"That's Taylor Adams. She owns Farmhouse Bakery."

"She's a baker? I wouldn't have called that. Hey, wait a minute. I know that place! I've been to her store! She's the one that makes those bagel doggie treats, isn't she?"

Jillian nodded. "Yes. She divorced her husband about the same time I lost Michael to cancer. That's how we met, at a support group."

"Roger that. She's a great baker. I love her croissants. Okay, who's that older guy they're talking to?"

"Seriously? Zack, you're incorrigible."

"What? What'd I say?"

"That's Zora Lumen. You've met her before."

I've said it before and I'll say it again. The 4th Street Gallery owner had to be the most masculine woman I have ever laid eyes on in my life. Gray hair pulled back in a tight ponytail, high forehead, prominent cheekbones, it was all there. The only thing she was missing was an Adam's apple. It also didn't help that she was wearing black slacks and a white long-sleeved blouse that looked remarkably like a buttoned down business shirt.

"Oh. Uh, my bad."

"Did you do that on purpose or did you actually think Zora was a man?"

"I still think Zora looks like a guy," I admitted. "Looks like a duck, quacks like a duck..." Jillian dug her nails into my arm, forcing me to change the subject. "Who's standing just behind Zora?"

"That would be Margaret Woodson. She's a teacher at the high school, too. She's the math teacher. I believe you know her son."

"I do?"

"Spencer. Goes by Woody."

I snapped my fingers, "That's right. He runs the hobby shop, doesn't he?"

"Yes. In fact, there he is. Looks like he's going to join his mother."

I saw Woody stroll up to his mother with an attractive young girl on his arm. I derisively shook my head. He was a little too old for her, I thought.

"Zoe looks lovely, doesn't she?" Jillian asked as she smiled at the young girl. The girl noticed she was being watched and waved back.

"Looks to be a little young for him, dontcha think?" I whispered. We had almost approached the little group and I didn't want them overhearing me.

"She's his daughter, you nitwit. Zoe is only

twelve. Get your mind out of the gutter."

"Proof positive that I couldn't guess a girl's age if my life depended on it," I offered, by way of apology.

I shook hands with Woody and met his family. Then it was right down the line, as though I was congratulating an opposing sports team on their victory after the game. Jillian's friends were polite and cordial. Hannah smiled wistfully at the two of us and had to look away. Taylor, once she learned I was the proud daddy of two corgis, made me promise I'd stop by her bakery for a complimentary baggie of doggie treats. She threatened to talk our ear off about Simon, her pet Manx cat, and all his zany exploits until thankfully Jillian noticed a few other people milling about and pulled us away. The only thing Zora did was to give me one of her creepy trademark smiles before eventually wandering off.

I met the mayor, his wife, and the town's district attorney. You want to talk about feeling out of place? I had absolutely nothing in common with these people. I caught the mayor throwing me curious glances every so often. Clearly he was familiar with my name and my brief, but colorful, history in his town.

Once there was a lull in the conversation, I suggested to Jillian that we should go and check out some of the exhibits. After all, we were here to see what curiosities had been set up, not to socialize. At least I was.

Let me take a moment to inform all the fine gents who might be reading this that you should never, ever suggest to a woman that she does too much socializing. Don't hint at it, don't suggest it, don't even insinuate it. However, if you decide to not pay heed to my advice, thankfully most towns have at least one florist shop.

I was about ready to pull her away from her small group of friends when I thought better of it. I risked a sidelong glance at Jillian. She's probably known these people her whole life. She'd be comfortable spending the entire evening renewing old acquaintances. As for me, I was curious to see what Egyptian Exhibitions had brought with them.

As we wandered the floor, we saw display cases filled with ancient broken tablets covered with Egyptian hieroglyphs spanning every square inch. We came across one of the tables that had been draped with black felt. A variety of sticks and broken wood had been tastefully arranged across the surface. Some had bits of metal on them while others had tiny figures carved onto various locations.

"What's with all the sticks?" I quietly asked Jillian.

"Tori told me a little about them. They're canes, even if they might not look like them. See the marks on that one there? Near the curved head? I can see a figure of Anubis. There's Osiris. Did you know that they found over 130 canes inside King Tut's tomb? I can't even imagine what one person is supposed to do with that many canes. Do you know how old these are?"

"Okay, I'll bite. How old?"

"Some are at least 3,000 years old! That's three millennia, Zack. Simply incredible."

We moved to the large glass case that had caught my eye the moment we stepped inside the auditorium. This case had several racks of jewelry. Large golden pendants festooned with chipped pieces of jade and sparkling colored glass met my eye. Glittering gold rings, tarnished silver brooches, and a wide variety of earrings were in the next case over and were prominently displayed for all to admire.

I caught sight of a table filled with swords and weapons. I gently tugged Jillian away from the jewelry and made our way over. I heard Jillian gently tsk me.

"Boys and their toys."

"How can you not want to look at a group of ancient weapons? Look at those swords. I can only imagine the battles they must have fought."

"Why, Zachary Anderson. I do believe you're having a good time."

I smiled and shrugged. I couldn't argue the point. I was surprised to learn that I enjoyed reading about ancient cultures. Seeing those battered and rusted swords had really got me thinking. As long as they didn't have a...

"I was really hoping to see a mummy," Jillian

wistfully said, interrupting me in mid-thought. I could only hope I was giving her a blank stare. "Can you imagine seeing an actual mummified person who lived thousands of years ago?"

I fought to suppress a shudder. No thinking was required to answer that question.

"I'd rather not."

"What? Why not?"

I thought back to all the countless monster movies I had watched as a child. Vampires, sea monsters, Frankenstein's creation, werewolves. Of all of them, the movies which had spooked me the most were those having anything to do with dead people. More specifically, dead decrepit forms rising slowly out of their sarcophagi. Halting steps. One leg being dragged limply along behind the other. Outstretched arms ... I shuddered again.

Look, I realize that it was completely irrational for me, a grown adult, to be spooked by mummies. Deep down, I knew full well that it was physiologically impossible for a mummified person to come back from the dead. Why, then, should I have a problem with them? Thankfully, I had already scanned the immediate area and was relieved to see that there weren't any caskets anywhere. To be completely honest, that was the first thing I did as soon as I stepped foot in the auditorium.

By this time, we had wandered over to a table adorned with jewelry. Jillian was staring at me with the beginnings of a smile on her face. I certainly hoped she couldn't tell I had a deep, irrational fear of mummies. The last thing I wanted to do was have to explain to her that I was afraid of breaking out into a cold sweat whenever the subject came up.

Thankfully, we heard the unmistakable sound of someone tapping on a microphone. Good. Saved by the bell. We both looked over at the stage. An older gentleman wearing a black tuxedo, and sporting a very dark tan, was standing before the podium. He continued to tap on the mic to get everyone's attention.

"Citizens of Pomme Valley. Good evening!"

There was a polite round of applause. People began moving to the dozens of rows of seating arranged before the stage. Jillian and I took our seats right next to Vance and Tori.

"We, the curators of the Egyptian Exhibitions, are delighted to be able to bring you a little piece of our Egyptian culture. I am Dr. Asiz Tarik, lead curator. Come with me as we explore the rich culture of the Eighteenth Dynasty of Egypt, a period of time stretching from circa 1533 to 1292 BC."

The good doctor cleared his throat and waited a few moments for a few stragglers who had just appeared to join the crowd. As soon as the two elderly couples had taken their seats, Dr. Tarik decided to continue.

"Ladies and gentlemen," Dr. Tarik was saying, "as many of you will know, the Eighteenth Dynasty is the most eminent of all the Egyptian dynasties. Why? Because it can boast that it included one of the most famous pharaohs of all time. Of course, I'm talking about none other than Tutankhamun, the boy king. As you may or may not recall, his tomb was discovered by the esteemed Howard Carter in 1922. Tutankhamun ruled from circa 1332 to 1323 BC. He ended up marrying his half-sister, Ankhesenpaaten, and had several daughters. They..."

Just then, we all heard a loud "Eww!" The lurid exclamation echoed noisily in the cavernous auditorium. Snickers and laughter ensued. Everyone looked around to see if they could tell who had said it. The problem was, it was me. In my defense, I hadn't shouted it, which is probably what you must have thought. I had said it in a normal voice, figuring it'd be drowned out by the curator's discussion. However, I made the mistake of saying that at the same time in which our esteemed host had paused for dramatic effect and the whole auditorium had fallen deathly quiet.

"Zachary!" Jillian hissed at me, shocked and appalled.

I'm sure my face was flaming red by this point.

"Umm, sorry? Pardon me."

The crowd continued to snigger at me. I risked a glance at Vance. He was shaking his head and laughing his rear off. Thankfully, Tori was laughing, too. After a minute or two, the laughter echoing throughout the auditorium died off.

"Continuing on," the curator said, stifling his own chuckle, "Tutankhamun and his wife had two daughters. Both were stillborn, I'm afraid."

The curator continued to talk about Tutankhamun's life, his accomplishments, and his reign. I heard about how Tut reversed several changes his father had made, moved the capital from one city to the next, and even ended the worshipping of one god, Aten, to restore another, Amun.

It wasn't until fifteen minutes later, when Dr. Tarik finally started talking about Tut's tomb, and the artifacts found within, that the evening began to pick up. Unfortunately for me, Jillian was going to get her wish. Turns out the good doctor brought an authentic mummy with him. While insignificant in nature, this mummy was one of five that had been discovered inside one of the smaller chambers inside KV62. For those of you that don't know what KV62 is, that's the official designation of Tut's tomb. Hey, it's okay. Up until a few minutes ago, I didn't know what that meant, either.

Much to my dismay, Dr. Tarik steered the discussion over to mummies and the Egyptian process of mummification. The process, Dr. Tarik explained, began with the complete evisceration of the body. Now, in case you're not familiar with the word, allow me to shed some light on its definition:

Eviscerate [verb ih-vis-uh-reyt; adjective ih-vis-er-it, -uh-reyt]

1. To remove the entrails from; disembowel

2. To deprive of vital parts

3. Surgery. To remove the contents of (a body part)

If that doesn't make you cringe, then this next part will. The removal of the brain. The brain was usually removed by way of a long, slightly hooked tool introduced through the nose. It was then swirled around a bit, liquefying the brain matter, and then the brain was poured out through the nose. Sound pleasant? I had to suppress a shudder. Apparently, according to the good doctor, it is not uncommon for the brain to be left in the mummy. However, that wasn't the case for this poor fellow.

The next step was to desiccate the body.

Desiccate [des-i-keyt]

1. To dry thoroughly; dry up

2. To preserve (food) by removing moisture; dehydrate.

"The deceased," Dr. Tarik lectured, "was laid out on a mound of natron salts—salts native to the area—and after a period of 35-70 days the salt would absorb all moisture. The flesh would shrink and the skin would darken."

Let me interrupt here and say that by now I was completely and thoroughly grossed out. A quick glance around the room confirmed I wasn't the only one. Flutes of champagne and plates of fancy hors d'oeuvres were quietly handed to the uniformed waiters who were unobtrusively moving through the crowds. I held out my own plate of Andouille sausage and crackers to a passing waiter. He grinned at me and took the plate without question.

"The final step," Dr. Tarik said, "was to remove the lungs, intestines, stomach, and liver. Once dried out they were placed in four separate canopic jars, one each for the four sons of Horus. For protection."

"What about the heart?" one woman asked from the audience.

"That's Maya Nelson," Jillian whispered in my ear. "She's married to the police chief."

"I remember him," I whispered back. "He didn't care for me too much. Trust me, the feeling was mutual."

Dr. Tarik smiled and nodded. "The heart. I am glad you asked about that. The heart had to remain in place. It was believed that it would testify for the deceased in the afterlife. A scarab, or sometimes a pendant, was often placed over the heart to protect the deceased in his voyage to the afterlife."

I leaned toward Vance.

"Remind me not to sign up to be mummified when I die."

Vance nodded. "Right there with you, pal."

"Hush," Tori scolded, throwing a frown at both of us.

"Sorry," Vance mumbled.

"Sorry," I added, at the same time.

Dr. Tarik then launched into more details about why more than one mummy was often-times discovered in the same tomb. One of the ways to show status was to be buried with your possessions. All your possessions, it would seem. And that, unfortunately, included slaves.

I shook my head in disbelief. Poor unlucky bastards. Your king dies and you're chosen to be mummified along with him? Talk about pissing off the wrong people.

Once more my mind drifted back to the monster movies I had seen when I was a kid. Considering my present circumstances, I really wished the mummies didn't creep me out as much as they did. Flashbacks of nightmares I had as a child came back to me. Shriveled, linen-wrapped crumbling fingers reaching out to me, desperate to wrap around my throat to squeeze the life out of me. Or suck all my fluids out so that it could be properly reanimated. Or...

I groaned, drawing a questioning look from Jillian. I gave her a shrug. I really did watch too many movies.

"Without further ado," Dr. Tarik was saying, "it gives me great pleasure to introduce the star of Egyptian Exhibitions, Meriptah, direct from KV62. Here he is!"

"He'd better be there," I quietly murmured.

"What was that?" Jillian softly inquired.

"The mummy. He'd better be there."

"Where else would he be? Gone?"

"Yeah, you know, like he wandered off or something."

"You heard what they did to mummies," Jillian reminded me. "I'm quite certain he'll be right where he's supposed to be."

There was a great splattering of applause as the red stage curtains were whisked away, revealing...

My stomach sank. I mean it literally felt like it suddenly dropped down to my toes. At the same time, a woman screamed. Actually, I was pretty certain it was Mrs. Nelson, the police chief's wife. Fingers began pointing. I quickly looked back at our host. Dr. Tarik's expression was not something I was ever going to forget. There was a look of utter shock on his face, which quickly switched to sheer terror.

Behind the curtain a golden sarcophagus—nowhere near as ornate as King Tut's—had been propped up at a forty-five degree angle, allowing the audience to look inside. The lid was open and everyone could see there wasn't any mummy nestled within. There were also five small glass display cases arranged in a semicircle behind the sarcophagus, displaying a variety of golden trinkets and sparkling jewelry. Well, four of them were. One of them had been smashed apart.

Dr. Tarik rushed over to the sarcophagus and explored the inside with his hands, as though he wasn't trusting what his eyes were telling him.

Then, catching sight of the destroyed case, he cried out in dismay and hurried over to inspect the damage. Just then, two men and one woman, dressed in identical dark green shirts and khaki pants, converged on the stage. They all gasped with surprise. Dr. Tarik gestured to the destroyed display.

"Good heavens! It's gone! The Nekhbet Pendant has been stolen!"

TWO

Jillian's surprised expression mirrored my own. Her shocked eyes met mine. She looked at me, back at the stage, and then back at me.

"How did you know that would happen?"

"I didn't," I insisted. "I was just joking!"

"Nobody touch anything!" Vance thundered, silencing the entire room. The detective rushed to the stage and clambered up the steps. "Nobody moves!"

Dr. Tarik looked up at Vance with an ashen face.

"Who—who are you?"

"Detective Vance Samuelson, PVPD."

Two more men hurried to the stage and joined the small group of people. One was older, portly, and balding. He looked winded from his brief sprint up the stairs. The other was much younger —around my age—and looked more uncomfortable in his tux than I did in mine. The three of them huddled together, just like a football team would do when trying to decide on a play. For several minutes they all huddled together, whispering amongst themselves. Suddenly Vance straightened, looked over at me, and then back at the older fellow. A few fingers were pointed my way.

"What's going on?" Jillian asked in a low voice.

"I wish I knew. I don't know why they're pointing at me. I had nothing to do with this."

After a few more minutes, the group broke apart. The older gentleman joined the others at the remains of the display case. The younger man headed to the open sarcophagus and inspected the insides. Vance again looked my way. His eyes briefly met mine before he looked over at Tori. He mouthed something, to which I saw her nod, and then looked back at me. What was he up to?

"Zack?" Vance's voice rang out. "Could you come up here and give me a hand?"

Heads swiveled until all eyes were locked on me. Caught like a deer in headlights, I blinked stupidly at my friend. Jillian nudged my shoulder.

"Vance needs your help. You'd better go on up there."

I threaded my way through the crowd of curious onlookers and made my way up the stairs. Dr. Tarik and his companions had returned to the smashed display case and were staring wordlessly at the broken glass. I approached Vance and gave him a questioning look.

"What do you need me to do?"

"Get with Don and Rick and help secure the school. No one gets in or out."

"Who's Don and who's Rick?" I asked, looking

back at the sea of unfamiliar faces.

The two men that had joined Vance on the stage suddenly appeared by his side. The older man approached first.

"Don Reezen," he announced, holding out a hand. "I'm principal of the school."

"Richard Werther," the other man added, also extending a hand. "I'm the vice principal here at PVHS."

I shook both of their hands. I glanced back at Vance, but he was already deep in conversation with Dr. Tarik. I pointed at the doors.

"I'm not sure what I can do, but I'm more than happy to help. Come on. We need to make sure no one leaves. If something was stolen, then we need to make certain it doesn't leave the premises. If it does, then who knows what type of curse will befall us."

Principal Reezen nodded and ignored my failed attempt to lighten the mood, "Agreed. Rick, grab every teacher you see. Post someone at every entrance into the school. I'll stand watch by the main entrance. We'll need someone at both the east and west school entrances. There are four doors leading into this auditorium. I want someone posted at each door. Oh, don't forget the loading bays in maintenance."

Richard nodded and hurried off.

"What should I do, Don?" I asked the principal. "You guys obviously know this school better than I do. I'm not even sure why Vance wanted my help."

"Come with me," Don curtly answered, pulling my arm to guide me toward the school's main entrance. "You were asked to help because of me, I'm sure. I've known Vance for years. His father and I are good friends. We speak all the time."

That drew me up short. We arrived at the main entrance where the principal began closing the six main doors, which had been propped open. I hurried over to the closest door, kicked the wedge of rubber that had been jammed under it to keep it from swinging shut, and moved to the next.

"Okay, that still doesn't explain why I'm here. You and I don't really know each other, right?"

Principal Reezen nodded. "Correct. However, I am a fan of your dogs. More specifically, Sherlock."

"My dogs?" I repeated, confused. "What about them? What do they have to do with anything?"

"Vance told me all about your case a few months ago," Don told me as he closed the last door. From one of his pockets, he retrieved a key ring that would make a janitor proud and began locking the doors. "I heard all about how your little dog kept locating clues where no one else could find any. He essentially kept you out of jail, did he not?"

I stared at the principal in shock. That's why he wanted me here? He wanted to see if Sherlock could shed any light on the missing mummy and the pendant? How was that going to look when all of a sudden a guy with a couple of corgis shows up and lets them sniff around the area? I could see the headlines now:

Dogs Send Local PD to Doghouse!

"Are you sure that's a wise idea?" I asked. "The local PD and I aren't exactly on the best of terms. If Sherlock can find clues where they cannot, do you have any idea how that's going to make them look?"

"The police can run their own investigation," Don informed me, dropping his voice down low.

A couple in their mid-fifties had appeared. They were headed toward the door. I moved to intercept.

"I'm sorry," I began, "but we all have to stay put until we're given the green light by the cops."

"By what cops?" the man asked, puzzled.

I was standing nearly six feet away from the guy and I could instantly smell what these two had been doing. A strong pungent, earthy aroma was emanating from these two. I instantly thought of skunk, but not as nauseous. I glanced over at the principal. I could see that his nostrils were flared. He smelled it, too.

"Been enjoying yourselves?" Principal Reezen asked, raising an eyebrow.

"Whatever do you mean?" the woman asked, trying to act confused.

"You two are a disgrace," Don muttered. "It's bad enough that you smoke marijuana, but to do so here? In a school? You know better than that."

Both heads fell.

"Go back and wait with the others," Principal Reezen ordered. "And I'd suggest you start praying that I don't press any charges."

"We're not students here," the man snapped. "And I have a legal prescription for it, so there."

"You both do?" I asked, looking over at the woman, who refused to look me in the eye.

"Be that as it may," Principal Reezen snapped, "marijuana is, by definition, a controlled substance. Under no circumstances whatsoever will controlled substances be permitted on school grounds. Now get with the others or I will have the police notified. What will it be?"

The couple hastily retreated, disappearing down the hall toward the auditorium.

"I really think we ought to let the police conduct their own investigation," I suggested as Principal Reezen locked the last door. "I don't want to get in their way."

"You won't be," Vance's voice broke in, startling me. I turned to watch the detective approach. "I've already spoken with the chief. Jerry and Rob —they would be our crime scene techs—are still in Portland at a conference. They've already been notified, but won't be here until tomorrow morning. So if you and Sherlock are gonna do your magic, it'll have to be tonight."

"Our magic?" I repeated. "Vance, for all we know, that was a one-time thing. There's no guarantee Sherlock can find anything."

"Let's give him the benefit of the doubt, shall we?" Vance suggested.

"What about Medford?" I protested. "Can't they send someone over to start processing this mess? I can't imagine the chief is okay with leaving this scene as it is, with a chance of it being tampered with."

"He's not. He's posting men here for the night to make sure no one bothers it. Besides, we've already tried. Medford has their people in Portland, too."

"Medford is much larger than PV," I persisted. "They must have techs to spare, don't they?"

"They have a large enough staff to leave one person behind," Vance confirmed. "However, he's tied up with an attempted bank robbery. They wouldn't be able to send him out until tomorrow, which is when our own guys will make it back. So for now, we have to wait."

"I also don't want to get you into any trouble," I added. "Wouldn't there be hell to pay if it became known that you allowed me and a couple of dogs inside an active crime scene?"

"It's easy," Vance explained. "Look, but don't touch. If you find anything, or should I say, if Sherlock finds anything then I'll pass it off as a discovery I made."

"And take the credit for something you didn't discover?" I asked, frowning as I said it.

"Would you like me to add Sherlock or Watson's name to the final report?" Vance asked, throwing in a healthy dose of sarcasm. "Look, Zack. I'm asking for your help. I know what this is going to do to Tori. She helped to push these people to bring their display to PV. I don't want any fingers to start pointing in her direction. She's already stressed enough. So, will you do me this favor? I'd like to see if there's anything Sherlock notices before the crime scene boys arrive tomorrow. Will you help me?"

"What about all the witnesses?" I asked, perplexed. "They're going to know you allowed a dog to come in here and check things out."

"Let's do this. Tori will take you and Jillian home. Come back here in about an hour, okay? I've called in two other cop friends of mine who will help me search the guests and lock everything down for the night. Then we'll let Sherlock do his thing."

I looked over the principal and raised an eyebrow.

"I must admit I am insanely curious to see if your dog finds anything," Don confessed.

"We're talking about a dog here, fellas," I reminded everyone. "A dog."

"A very smart dog," Vance added, drawing a nod from the principal. "Go. There's Tori and Jillian. Be back here in an hour."

* * *

Almost an hour later, I pulled my Jeep up to the high school. I saw a couple of cop cars parked outside. Several strips of yellow crime scene tape were stretched across each of the school's six entry doors. I unloaded the dogs and hesitantly approached the police officer who had been watching me ever since I parked.

"You must be Zack," the officer said. "I'm Eric Knudsen." He squatted down to pet Sherlock and Watson, who were both gazing up at the strange man with rapt fascination. "Which one is Sherlock?"

"Him," I said, pointing at the tri-color corgi. "He's the one with black on him. Watson is the red and white."

"Hello, Sherlock." The cop held out a hand. Sherlock rewarded the kind gesture with a lick. "I've heard a lot about you. I hope you're able to find something, buddy. Watson? Your other dog is named Watson? That's clever."

I smiled. "Thanks. I'm surprised. I would have thought you'd want the cops to take credit for the case, not a pair of dogs."

Eric looked left, then right. He lowered his voice to a whisper.

"Between you and me? Both of the crime scene techs are pains in the butt. Just because they're CSTs they think they're better than everyone else. I personally would love to see them knocked down a peg or two."

"Whatever happened to team spirit?" I asked.

"It went right out the window when Jerry insinuated I belong directing traffic. Pompous prick."

That was all the convincing I needed.

"Sherlock? Let's go do your thing. Come on, Watson."

Eric lifted the strip of crime scene tape and allowed me to duck under to enter the school. The hallways were illuminated, as though I expected to hear a bell ring at any minute. Doors would bang open, kids would begin screaming, and then there'd be nothing but chaos running rampant through the halls until the bell sounded again, signaling the beginning of the next class.

Ah. To be back in high school. I wouldn't wish that on my worst enemy. It was hard enough to be a kid, and even more so nowadays. There was pressure to maintain your grades, pressure to not fall in with the wrong crowds, pressure to spend time with your family, and, for the older kids, pressure to find a job so that they could earn some spending money. All I had to worry about when I was that age was to keep my grades up. Even then, I never worried about it too much. I had always received good grades. They probably could have been better had I studied more. Then again, I was a teenager. I already thought I knew everything.

At the moment, though, the hallways were empty. My footfalls echoed noisily as I retraced my steps from earlier in the evening back to the auditorium. The hall I was following was lined with a double row of small lockers. I hesitated only long enough to inspect the size. I swear the lockers I used back in my school in Arizona were twice the size of these. I doubted these would hold more than three or four books each.

Sherlock tugged on his leash. He sniffed loudly and lifted his nose into the air. Watson turned to give him a questioning look. Moments later she, too, had her nose in the air and was pulling on her leash. Did the dogs smell something? Had Sherlock already zeroed in on some type of clue? Both corgis were pulling on their leashes, threatening to drag me along whether I wanted to accompany them or not.

I led the corgis into the auditorium. Vance and a second man I didn't recognize were there, chatting with a very harassed Dr. Tarik. The three of them turned to watch us approach.

"Is this some kind of joke?" Dr. Tarik sputtered. "I was expecting to see an officer with a genuine police dog. But this? Did you borrow those two from Her Royal Majesty the Queen? What business have they in a crime scene?"

"I'll vouch for both the guy and the dogs," Vance gently told him. "You're upset, I get that. Let us do our job, okay?"

We were waved over.

"Zack, this is Dr. Asiz Tarik, head curator at Egyptian Exhibitions. Dr. Tarik, this is a friend of mine, Zack Anderson. Down there are Sherlock and Watson."

"I am still not amused," Dr. Tarik said, rather gruffly.

I shook the doctor's hand. His skin was weathered and calloused. The grip was firm and unfaltering. This was a man who spent a lot of time outdoors.

"Nice to meet you," I offered.

"What are your qualifications?" Dr. Tarik immediately asked.

"I'm a writer," I answered.

Dr. Tarik threw his hands up in the air.

"Isn't it just like you Americans? Let me venture a guess. You have watched too many of your American police television shows and you now think you are an expert on the matter. No offense to you, Mr. Anderson, but I want a professional here."

Vance scowled. "As you wish, Dr. Tarik. You may leave now."

The curator puffed out his chest and several veins appeared on his forehead.

"Excuse me? I will do no such thing. I can see now that it was a mistake to come to this little town. We were assured we would have adequate security to protect our collection. Where is that teacher? The one who campaigned to bring Egyptian Exhibitions here? I'll wager she knows something about what has happened."

"Whoa," Vance snapped. "Cool your jets, buddy. If you're insinuating that Tori Samuelson is somehow responsible for this mess, then you are dead wrong."

The curator's angry face swung over to the

Vance's.

"Do not take that tone with me, detective," Dr. Tarik said, throwing as much venom as he could into his voice. "I am a distinguished archaeologist and am at the top of my profession. What about you?"

"Why you ...!" Vance snarled, taking a few menacing steps toward the curator.

Sherlock started barking. Watson added her two cents for every fourth or fifth bark of Sherlock's. I decided an intervention was in order before Vance ended up doing something that would get him kicked off the force. Or someone's ankle was bitten. I inserted myself between the two glaring men and held up my hands in surrender.

"Gentlemen, please. Vance, get a grip. Relax. We have bigger fish to fry. Dr. Tarik? Take it easy. We're trying to help you. I know it doesn't look like it, but Sherlock has a unique ability in locating clues. Let us look around. I would even encourage you to come with us. That way you'll see that we won't touch anything we're not supposed to."

The simple request of being allowed to accompany us took much of the wind out of his sails. The doctor's angry red face softened and he finally nodded. He looked down at the dogs and actually smiled.

"Very well. You may look, just don't touch."

I nodded and offered a smile in return, "No problem. Sherlock? Watson? Let's go look around, shall we?"

I led the dogs to the open sarcophagus first. Sherlock lowered his nose to the ground and sniffed along the base of the casket, moving left. Watson mirrored his actions, only she moved to the right. As you may have expected, both corgis came to an abrupt halt when my arms couldn't extend away from my sides any farther than they already were. Both arms were yanked in opposite directions.

"Ouch, guys. Really? Is that how we're going to play this? Pick a direction. Left, right, I don't care, only pick the same direction."

Sherlock turned to look at Watson. Almost immediately Watson changed course and followed Sherlock. Together they circled the entire casket. Sherlock then moved to the broken case.

"Careful, boy," I cautioned, drawing up the slack in his leash. I didn't want him treading over broken glass. "You're not getting any closer than that."

Sherlock sniffed once and then turned to look at the squat black wooden display stand. He stretched his neck up and over the large pieces of broken glass and nudged the base with his nose. He turned to look at me and then looked pointedly back at the base.

Vance, who had been watching intently, gingerly approached the broken display case and squatted down low. I stepped away from the case and pulled the two dogs close. Vance stared at the display stand then back and Sherlock.

"Alright, what about it?"

"You talk to the dogs, too?" Dr. Tarik skeptically asked.

"Awwooooo!" Sherlock howled.

It was low and quiet, and surprisingly enough, wasn't directed at the detective. I looked over at the curator, as did Vance. Dr. Tarik, to his credit, was smiling as he looked down at Sherlock. He extended a hand, which Sherlock sniffed, then licked.

"Was your dog howling at me?" the curator asked, still watching Sherlock. "I see why the queen is so infatuated with the breed. I will admit they are adorable."

Watson approached, sat, and lifted a paw.

"Very well. You are not to be overlooked, kind sir."

Watson blinked her eyes as she returned the stare.

"Watson is a 'she'," I told Dr. Tarik.

"You named her Watson?" the curator asked, baffled. "That is a name for a male, not a female."

Vance gave me a triumphant look, "Hah!"

"Shut up, dude," I said. Both corgis turned to look at me. Sherlock's expression was more piteous while Watson had nothing but loving adoration in her eyes. "We'll get into that later. Right now we need to find out why he's looking at the wooden base there."

Vance straightened and slowly walked around the wooden stand. On the flip side of the case, the part that was hidden from the audience's view, Vance stopped. He squatted, peered closely at something, and then absently patted his pockets. He was still wearing his tuxedo. He clearly didn't have whatever gear he usually carried with him.

"What do you need?" I asked. "What do you see?"

"There's a tiny strip of something here," Vance reported, pointing at the base of the stand. "The stand has a small split in the wood. It looks like something has snagged in it. I wanted a pair of tweezers so I could pull it out."

I patted my belt. I had my handy-dandy multi-tool—complete with a pair of needle-nose pliers—tucked away in its pouch on my belt. I pulled it out and unfolded the tool, almost like I was whipping out a butterfly knife. The pliers appeared. I presented it, handle first, to the detective.

"Here. Use this. I always carry this thing. Will it work?"

Vance took the tool and studied it.

"Well, it isn't tweezers, but it'll do. Let's see what we have here."

He gingerly pulled the tiny scrap of material from the split in the wood and held it up for a closer inspection. I watched Dr. Tarik squat down next to the detective. His eyes opened wide.

"Where did you get that?" the curator demanded.

Vance pointed out the tiny imperfection in the wood base.

"Right there. Why? Do you know what this is?"

Dr. Tarik nodded. He immediately looked over at the open sarcophagus. I groaned and felt the blood drain from my face. Was he thinking what I think he was thinking?

"This is a scrap of linen from Meriptah. Look. The linen has been coated with resin. This came from a mummy."

Vance gave the curator a neutral look and cleared his throat.

"Are you trying to tell me that the mummy woke up, ambled over here, broke the display case open, and stole some necklace?"

"Pendant," Dr. Tarik corrected. "I know how this looks and how it sounds. For the record, that's not what I'm suggesting at all. However, no one knew about the pendant. It is very famous, worn by King Tut himself! It is completely irreplaceable. We must get it back!"

"Talk to me about that pendant," Vance told the curator. "What's so valuable about it?"

Dr. Tarik's voice lowered to a whisper. Vance and I crowded close so we could hear him.

"As I mentioned earlier, mummies are wrapped in multiple layers of linen fortified with resin after every two layers of bandages. It is not uncommon to find objects on the mummy at different layers."

"How many" I asked.

Dr. Tarik shrugged. "It varies. Beads, pendants, scarabs, weapons..."

JEFFREY POOLE

"No," I interrupted. "What I meant was, how many different layers do the mummies have?"

"Oh. My apologies. As many as twenty alternating layers of bandages have been counted. The innermost layers of a mummy typically contain the deceased's possessions. The Nekhbet Pendant had been discovered around the king's neck in the innermost wrappings. Most likely it means Tutankhamun wore it on his person when he was alive. Do you understand the significance of this? Its loss to the academic world is incalculable. It must be returned. Detective, you must prevail!"

"What does this missing pendant look like?" Vance asked.

I nodded. It was a good question. I was curious, too.

Overhearing the detective's question, one of the other curators approached, holding an open book. Dr. Tarik's eyes lit up as soon as he saw it.

"Excellent, Ammar. Thank you. Gentlemen, here is a picture of Nekhbet's Pendant."

I whistled with admiration. While not a fan of the Egyptian style of jewelry in general, I had to admit that it was an exquisite piece of work. I was looking at a picture of a vulture with its wings partially extended and the tips folded down. The top of the pendant, a surprisingly realistic depiction of an avian head, was turned to the left. There were also some type of red gem clutched in each of its talons. Sherlock stretched his neck up and whined. If I didn't know any better, I'd say he wanted a look, too.

Surprisingly, Dr. Tarik dropped to one knee and lowered the book down to Sherlock's level. The inquisitive corgi sniffed once and then returned to sniffing the ground. The curator held the book out to Watson, but she didn't seem to care one way or the other.

"For a vulture, it's a pretty looking thing," I decided.

Vance nodded with agreement.

"This pendant is a representation of the vulture goddess, Nekhbet," Dr. Tarik patiently explained. "It is solid gold and encrusted with blue glass. You'll no doubt note how realistic the head appears. Its eyes are of obsidian and the beak is lapis lazuli. The red you see here is more colored glass."

"Are those rubies in its talons?" I asked, tapping the bird's feet.

"Carnelian," Dr. Tarik answered.

"How big is it?" Vance asked.

"From wing tip to wing tip it's about five inches across and nearly three inches high."

"So it's a good-sized sucker," Vance observed thoughtfully.

"Your impressive use of American colloquialism continues to astound me," Dr. Tarik groaned.

"Small wonder, seeing how we're in the United States of America, buddy," Vance muttered crossly. "Listen, doc, why in the world did you have a priceless valuable like that pendant in an exhibit like this? Weren't you worried about something like this happening?"

"Of course," Dr. Tarik said, nodding. "As a matter of fact, it was on its way to a new facility. We thought transporting this in such a manner would have been enough to dissuade anyone from trying to steal it. You have to understand, no one knew of its history. No one knew it was authentic."

"Wait a minute," I said, growing angry. "Do you mean to say that none of these things in here are authentic? What are you trying to do, pull one over on us?"

"Egyptian Exhibitions has never once claimed that any of the artifacts in its possession were authentic. We utilize highly accurate reproductions in our exhibit. Our organization's sole purpose is to educate and entertain the general public."

I looked over at Vance to see what his reaction to that revelation was. For the record, he looked as shocked as I felt. After a few moments his frown disappeared.

"That's why you had the pendant. It should have been the perfect way to transport the piece from one museum to another without fear of its true nature becoming known."

"What better hiding place could there be than placing it in the open?" Dr. Tarik agreed.

"How many people had access back here?" Vance wanted to know.

"Only myself," Dr. Tarik confirmed. "I never told anyone, not even my assistant, Ammar. The fewer people who knew the truth, the better."

"How long had those curtains been closed?" Vance asked, looking over at the thick red curtains on either side of the stage. "I need to know how long these things back here had been left alone."

"We finished setting up the displays late yesterday," Dr. Tarik answered, eliciting a groan from Vance. "But, the artifacts in these cases had only been there for a few hours at most before the grand opening."

I cleared my throat.

"I hate to point out the obvious, but does it, or does it not, look like the mummy took the pendant?"

"Far be it for me to dispute your American cinema," Dr. Tarik dryly began, "but mummies do not come to life and they most certainly do not steal pendants."

"Hey, I'm not saying it did, okay? Everyone is thinking it; I'm just stating it."

"I'm not thinking it," Vance disagreed.

"Nor am I," added Dr. Tarik.

I sighed and pointed at the scrap of linen Vance still held.

"Then explain that," I demanded.

"It had to have been planted there," Vance told me. "Someone wants us to think that the mummy did it. What do you have against mummies, anyway?"

"Nothing," I answered, albeit a tad too hastily.

Vance eyed me speculatively.

"Afraid the mummy is gonna getcha?"

"Ha, ha."

Sherlock suddenly tugged at his leash. He was looking at the back left corner of the stage. The inner workings of the platform were outlined in black fabric. Less noticeable to the audience, I presume. However, I thought I could make out a door against the wall. I let Sherlock lead the way, with Watson following closely behind him. I heard movement behind me. A quick look back confirmed Vance and Dr. Tarik were shadowing me.

"What do you want to look at, Sherlock?" I quietly asked the corgi. "Do you smell something back here?"

Sherlock dropped his nose to the ground, sniffed a few times, then headed straight toward the door. I glanced back at Vance.

"Do I open it?"

Vance grinned. "Sure, unless you're afraid something is going to jump out at you from the shadows."

"Jerk. Bite me."

I heard Vance laugh. Opening the door revealed a darkened hallway stretching twenty feet to the left and about that same distance to the right. There were three doors on the right-hand side of the hall if I chose left, and there was one door each on the right and the left if I chose to go right.

Sherlock tugged on the leash. He wanted to go left. Left it is. I was led to the last door on the right, which was a large double door. I looked through the windows to see what was on the other side. Nothing, unfortunately. The lights were off. Sherlock turned to look up at me. I, in turn, looked over at Vance, who indicated I should open it. It was locked.

"Can't open this one," I reported.

Vance pulled out a huge ring of keys. I had seen that exact same key ring before. It belonged to the principal.

"Don let me borrow these," he explained as he fished through the keys to find one that worked. After a few minutes of fruitless searching, he found the correct key.

Once the door was open, and the lights were turned on, we could see that we were standing in another corridor. There were doors everywhere. I saw two on the left and at least four, no, better make that five on the right. The hall extended straight ahead for about ten feet then angled to the left and proceeded another dozen or so feet.

There were doors along this part of the hallway, too, but Sherlock ignored them. He led me straight to the end of the hall and then plopped his butt down on the linoleum. Watson, unsure what we were doing in this strange environment, kept looking up at me as if to verify I hadn't lost my marbles. I ruffled her fur and turned to watch Vance and the curator approach. The detective was already fumbling for his keys.

"Why are we here, again?" Dr. Tarik asked.

"What is the significance of this door?"

"Not a clue," I admitted.

"Is it locked?" Vance asked as he pulled the fat ring of keys from his tuxedo pocket.

"Probably. Let me check. I ... hmm. No, it's unlocked. Check it out."

I pushed open the door and then fumbled inside for a light switch. Properly illuminated, I could see that we were in some type of utility/storage room. The floor sloped inward, toward a recessed grate set into the ground in the middle of the room. The problem, however, was that the grate had been pulled from the ground. It—and a few broken tiles—was lying several feet away, as if it had been carelessly discarded after it had been yanked from the floor.

I stared at the dark opening as my mind spun into overdrive.

"Umm..."

"It's just a coincidence," Vance assured me. "Keep it together, princess."

"That's it. Sherlock, attack! Bite him in the ankles! Watson ... do your thing."

"Do what thing?" Vance wanted to know.

"It's better if I don't tell you," I cryptically told him.

"Americans are odd," Dr. Tarik decided.

Vance knelt down by the opening in the floor and peered inside. As he was straightening back up, he slid his hands along a length of one side of the hole. The detective froze as he ran his hand over the same section, and then a third time. He squatted back down for a closer inspection. A hand disappeared into one of his jacket pockets and reappeared, holding my multi-tool. He carefully picked a couple of fibers from the ground and held them up. He wordlessly held them out to the curator, who leaned forward to take a closer look.

"They are the same fibers as what we found at the destroyed display case," Dr. Tarik confirmed. "What does this mean?"

I sighed. I know what you're thinking. I must be one gullible dumb-cluck for even thinking the mummy could be responsible for this. However, there were scraps of ancient linen back on the platform and now several more had been discovered here. On top of which, there was an opening large enough for a human, not to mention a shriveled-up mummy to pass through. I knew full well that mummies couldn't come back to life, but then again, what else would fit the facts? What was that quote from Sherlock Holmes?

When you have eliminated the impossible, whatever remains, however improbable, must be the truth.

I glanced down at Sherlock. He was already watching me. Did he know what I was thinking? I looked over at Watson. She was busy watching Vance. Of course, the detective always seemed to be slipping the dogs some type of biscuit whenever he saw them, so I couldn't blame her.

We were stooped over the hole in the floor, each lost in silent contemplation, when there was a bang, followed almost immediately by a loud voice. Naturally, it had appeared from behind us.

"Whatcha doing back here?"

"JESUS H. CHRIST!" Vance bellowed, jerking back so violently he tripped over the fallen grate and fell to the ground.

Dr. Tarik cursed in his native language, clapping a hand over his heart. He quickly slapped his other hand over his mouth. "A thousand apologies. I should not have said that."

As for me, I had sucked in a breath and had been ready to shout out an expletive worthy of the situation when I caught sight of the dogs. Both had turned around and were panting contentedly at the intruder. Neither was surprised. In fact, both were happy to see the gate crasher.

It was Tori.

"Hon-ey!" Vance whined as he painfully rose to his feet. "What the heck! Why'd you do that?"

"You three sure are jumpy," Tori observed.

She had since changed from her evening gown into a baggy sweatshirt and jeans. I also noticed the soles of her shoes were thick and cushioned, thus enabling her to move about without being detected. Tori squatted down to throw an arm around each of the dogs.

"How are my two favorite corgis in the whole wide world?"

Both stumpy tails threatened to wag right off

their respective canine derrieres.

"What are you doing here, Tori?" Vance wanted to know, coming up to give his wife a hug. "It's not safe for you here."

"I wanted to help out," Tori explained. "I couldn't just sit at home, doing nothing."

"What about the kids?" Vance asked.

Tori shrugged. "Oh, you know, I just pulled some random stranger in a hockey mask off the street and asked him to put away the machete for the night. My kids needed watching, so I told him to make himself useful."

Alarmed, Dr. Tarik looked at me. I smiled and shook my head, indicating it was an inside joke between the two of them. The curator shook his head in bewilderment and let the matter drop.

"I assume you got Rachel to watch them?"

Rachel was their neighbor and good friend. I should know. Jillian introduced us last month when the Samuelsons hosted a neighborhood block party. Jillian and I, along with Sherlock and Watson, had been invited.

"Obviously. Now, what are you doing back here?"

Vance pointed at Sherlock.

"We're all following..."

Vance trailed off as Sherlock suddenly looked back down the hall—the way we had all come in —and softly woofed. Alarmed, I looked at Vance. Tori hurried to his side.

"Who else is in here?" I asked.

"No one," Vance assured me. "There are two officers stationed outside, but that's it. Tori, did you see anyone else on your way in here?"

Tori shook her head no. Together, we all looked down at Sherlock.

"What is it, boy?" I asked the tri-colored corgi, dropping my voice to a whisper.

Sherlock woofed again. The hairs on the back of his neck were standing up. Watson, who up until this point hadn't given any indication that she had noticed anything unusual, started growling.

I stared at Watson with shock written all over my features. I have never heard that quiet, timid little corgi growl at anything. Something was up. Something had spooked them.

Sherlock barked once and lunged forward. The little snot caught me just as I was transferring the leashes from one hand to the other. Caught off guard, Sherlock's leash was yanked out of my hand. Without a moment to lose, Sherlock bolted for the door. Watson tried the same trick, but by that time I already had a tight grip on her leash. She looked back at me, gave a high-pitched yip, and pulled on her leash. The meaning came through loud and clear. She wanted to go after her pack mate.

I quickly handed her leash to Tori while Vance and I took off after Sherlock. We made it to the end of the hall just in time to see one of the double doors swing shut. Confused, I looked over at

Vance. Besides Sherlock, who had just gone out the door? There's no way Sherlock could have opened that door by himself. Who was he chasing?

Memories of all the monster movies I had ever seen flooded back to me. Never once, in any one of them, did the story end well when someone went chasing after the monster. Deep down I knew that there was no way on earth an actual mummy could be responsible for this. Well, let's just say I was ninety-nine percent sure. However, it was that teeny tiny one percent that concerned me. My overactive imagination was in overdrive at the moment and it wouldn't shut up. What if it was the mummy? What if it grabbed Sherlock? What if it tried coming after me?

Vance and I burst through the double doors, both doors slamming open in opposite directions at the same time.

"Which way?" Vance asked. He turned to look right while I looked left.

"That way," I said, pointing left. I could hear the tell-tale click of doggie toe nails on a hard floor.

Vance sprinted past me.

"Hurry! Sherlock is after someone!"

"You noticed the doors, too?" I asked, trying not to wheeze. For crying out loud I wasn't that much out of shape, was I?

"Yes. Move your rear, Zack! There's someone in here besides us! We need to find out who!"

We angled left and saw a long straight corridor in front of us. Movement from our left attracted our attention. Another door was swinging shut. Sherlock started barking. He was inside that room. Vance and I barged through the door. It was some type of music room. I saw music stands, shelves of sheet music, and a professional looking percussion set on the far wall. Chairs had been set out in a semi-circle, facing the doors we had just come through.

Vance hit the first row of chairs and went down with a loud crash. I was about ready to help him up when Sherlock barked nearby. We were in one of those rooms that, even if you turned out the overhead lights, one or two fixtures remained lit. For safety's sake, I presume. Each was doing its best to illuminate the cavernous room, but it was only enough to allow me to see the general shape of the room.

Sherlock barked again. My head jerked up just as something was hurled through a window in the far corner of the room. A form suddenly rushed by me and flung itself through the opening. I was able to see tattered strips of ancient linen flapping through the air before it disappeared from sight. I rushed over to the window to peer anxiously out into the night. Whatever it was had vanished.

I heard a distinctive canine snort nearby. I also heard a groan coming from behind me. I gave Vance a hand in standing up while I looked back at the corner window. I found the closest light switch and flicked on the lights. There was Sherlock, slowly sniffing his way around the circumference of the room. He paused only long enough to give me a smug look.

"Are you okay?" I asked my friend.

"Smashed both knees on the way down," Vance groaned. "That hurt. A lot. What happened?"

"Uh…"

"Oh, come on, pal. You can't possibly say what I think you're gonna say."

THREE

T he following morning the dogs and I were on our way to Cookbook Nook to help Jillian get ready for Cider Fest. She had talked incessantly about how excited she was for the upcoming harvest festival. Now that it was finally here, she couldn't wait to visit the farms, sample the food each of the farms were going to offer, and so on. Turns out this was an event all of PV looked forward to each and every year.

In case you need a refresher course in French, the 'Pomme' in Pomme Valley translates to 'Apple', turning the literal translation of my hometown into Apple Valley. As you might have guessed, that means this town has apple farms galore. Turns out once a year PV holds a three-month long harvest festival—appropriately named 'Cider Fest'—celebrating anything having to do with that juicy red fruit. Roadside fruit stands popped up overnight. Every half a mile or so, around every bend in the road, was a mini farmers' market.

I also should clarify that we're not just talking

apples. Pears, apricots, peaches, oranges, lemons, and a myriad of assorted fruit also beckoned invitingly. The enticing aroma of freshly picked fruit is usually all it takes for me to stop and make a few selections. There are also bags of pistachios, sunflower seeds, pecans, walnuts, and almonds. Many of the shops inside the individual farms also stocked fresh preserves, canned fruit, candy, and baked goods.

Oh, the baked goods. I mustn't forget that sweet manna from heaven. Holy cow. Fresh, ready-to-bake apple pies, or berry pies, or turnovers, or ... Do you know what I found in one of the coolers, just waiting—begging—to be purchased? A twenty-pound Dutch apple pie. Did you get that? Twenty pounds! That's 20#, or 20lbs, or 'one honkingly humongous pie'! Who in their right mind needs a pie that big? You'd have to be cooking for at least a dozen people, if not more.

Of course I bought one.

Last Saturday, in anticipation of Cider Fest's grand opening this weekend, Jillian took me to one of the largest farms, Greentree Gardens. This sprawling farm covered hundreds of acres and was the farthest from town. According to Jillian, Greentree Gardens typically opened two weeks earlier than the competition, due to the simple fact that there was more to do and set up. Of course, it couldn't hurt that the farm typically hired several dozen seasonal workers to help them out, most of which were high school kids.

I remember pulling up to the long driveway to the farm and seeing several neighboring pastures in the process of being converted into parking lots. Teams of kids were roping off lots, marking spaces, and removing rocks, branches, and anything else most cars typically hate. I whistled in amazement. From the looks of things, they would be able to easily accommodate a hundred cars. I had to wonder what the appeal was. Why would they need that many parking spaces? Was their fruit that good?

Turns out the people weren't just coming for the freshly picked fruit. As I mentioned earlier, most farms had a variety of other products to sell. Not only did Greentree Gardens have fruit, nuts, preserves, and freshly baked goods, but they also had some type of craft fair. As many as forty 10 x10 foot tents had been set up in four rows of ten each. The vendors offered everything from delicate hand painted eggs to oil paintings. I saw an impressive collection of silver jewelry in one tent while another had cutting boards of all shapes and sizes. Luckily for us, most vendors had already set up shop. In fact, we had stopped at the tent where the cutting board vendor had just finished unpacking his wares and was settling down to enjoy his coffee.

"Good morning!" a friendly older gentleman announced, abandoning the crossword puzzle he had just pulled out. "Can I interest you in one of these fine bamboo cutting boards?"

"Did you make all these yourself?" I asked, amazed.

The shopkeeper proudly nodded. "I did. These were all hand made by me. Hello, Jillian."

Jillian smiled. "Hi, Max. Max, this is Zack Anderson. Zack, this is Max Steadwell. He's been making these cutting boards for as long as I can remember. Max, I've always wanted to ask you something."

"And what would that be?" Max asked, as he smiled and shook my hand.

"Who is your supplier of bamboo?"

Just then Max looked down and noticed that both Jillian and I were holding leashes.

"Ah! Would one of these two be the famous Sherlock I've heard so much about?"

I pointed over at Sherlock, who was returning the shopkeeper's gaze.

"That's him. And this is Watson," I added, pointing down at the little red and white corgi who was, at present, gazing up at me and wondering why we stopped.

Max retrieved a familiar bag of bagel dough doggie bits and offered a couple to each of the dogs. Seriously, did everyone have a bag of those things handy? Taylor Adams must be making a killing in this town.

"To answer your question, Jillian," Max said as he straightened back up and tossed the bag of treats on the table, "I can't speak for my competitors but as for me, I harvest what I need from my own farm."

"You grow your own bamboo?" I asked, impressed.

"It's easier than you think," Max assured me. "Once you get the bamboo started it grows like wildfire. To tell the truth I've got so much of it that I sell the surplus off to anyone who wants it. I've seen it made into furniture, mats, even clothes."

"You've got a lot of cool designs," I observed as I looked around the inside of his tent. "I see states, animals, fish, geometric shapes, and so forth."

"Do you have any dogs?" Jillian asked as she looked down at Sherlock.

Max nodded. "I do. They're over there, next to the Pacific Northwest states. Is there any breed in particular you're looking for? No, wait. Don't answer that. That was a foolish question."

The shopkeeper hurried over to the table and moved a few trays around. He slid a large bin over and started flipping through the boards, as though he was flipping through a crate of vinyl records. Max gave a grunt and slid one board out and presented it to us. It was a full body profile of a corgi, complete with a nub of a tail.

I grinned. "I'll take it."

"All of my boards feature formaldehyde-free glues, so you never have to worry about anything leeching into your food," Max explained, as he wrapped up the board.

I looked over at Jillian and shrugged. "Good to

know."

I thanked Max and we continued our tour. This farm was so huge that they had their own trout-stocked fishing pond, if I cared to try my hand at fishing. I didn't. I'm no fisherman. I'd get squeamish if I had to jab a hook through a poor worm's eye. Blech.

They also had pony rides—which would open in a few days—for the children and an actual eatery, in case you wanted something besides fruit. It looked like someone had simply parked a food truck nearby and built a wooden ramp and deck right next to it. Any way you looked at it, these people took their festivals seriously.

But I digress. As I was saying, my day had started early when Jillian called asking for help. She said she had brought in several boxes of decorations from home and needed some help setting everything up in her store. Here was a lady, I decided after Jillian informed me she had ten boxes waiting to be hauled in from her SUV, who enjoyed decorating. Everything was labelled. Everything had its place. Entire themed displays were stored in separate boxes and were carefully unpacked. She was not only decorating for the festival, she explained, but also for Halloween, which was less than a month away.

Now Halloween is a holiday I can get on board with. I love the spooky decorations. I love the candy. I love the cooler temps at night. I really love the candy. I love seeing people dressed up and having a good time.

Did I mention I love the candy?

No, believe it or not, I don't have a sweet tooth. You might be thinking otherwise after hearing about my fascination with candy. What can I say? There's something about walking into a room and seeing an open candy dish filled to the brim with assorted goodies that makes me smile. I like walking by said candy dish and snagging one when no one is watching, pretending like the calories I'm about to ingest don't count. Which, let's face it, on holidays they don't.

Three hours later, after we had finished setting up round one of Jillian's decorations, the dogs and I were running errands. Jillian had gone home to get a few more things so we decided to take advantage of our free time. We were just leaving Gary's Grocery, having turned left onto Stagecoach Drive, when Sherlock jumped up on his seat and started sniffing the air. I groaned. Had Watson dropped another bomb on us? I cautiously took a few sniffs of my own and kept my finger hovering over the controls to the windows in case an emergency venting was necessary. No, she hadn't, thank heavens. So what had attracted Sherlock's attention?

We passed by Gary's Grocery almost immediately after passing the giant wooden "Pomme Valley Welcomes You!" sign. To this day, I don't know how it took me so long to find the grocery store. There it was, sitting out in the open with a huge parking lot all around it. Yet, I distinctly remember that I spent nearly an hour driving around town looking for it. And there, on the corner, was PV's one and only convenience store, Square L.

I never could understand why a town this size would have both the grocery store and the convenience store in the same parking lot. Why not put it on the west side of town, so people heading east into PV could have a convenient place to stop and fuel up? I could only assume it was attributed to some type of zoning issue.

I kept scanning the immediate surroundings, looking for some indication of what Sherlock had been barking at. Naturally, by this time the little corgi had fallen silent. I shrugged and let the matter drop.

As I was driving down Main Street, I noticed that the city had its maintenance crews busy decorating for Cider Fest and for Halloween. Large fuzzy orange and black spiders were being suspended from lamp posts. Purple lights were being strung around windows. Fake cobwebs were stretched across street signs. All in all, everywhere I looked I could see people getting into the spirit of this festival. From the looks of things, everyone in PV got in on the act and decorated their stores to some degree.

I was approaching an orange road sign that wasn't there thirty minutes ago. It was a transportation notice, stating that Main Street was going to be closed for several hours a day for the next week or so. What would they possibly need to do that for? What were they planning on doing, holding a parade? How? Main Street was less than a quarter of a mile long. Trying to host a parade here in PV would be like trying to land a 747 in a parking lot. There just wasn't enough room.

For some inexplicable reason, my thoughts drifted back to the events of last night. I recalled the look of terror on Dr. Tarik's face once he saw that the mummy was gone. He had later denied it, but I had seen the fear in his eyes. For a moment, however brief it had been, the good doctor had believed the mummy had been responsible for the theft of the necklace.

The necklace. What had the doctor called it? Nekhbet's Pendant? I remembered the picture of that jeweled vulture thing I had been shown last night. Had King Tut really worn that when he had been alive? If so, wouldn't that allow the necklace to fall into the uber-rare 'priceless' category? How much would the right collector be willing to pay for it? What other treasures might the mummy, er, perpetrator be after? All this talk and speculation about Egyptology had me eager to learn more.

I looked at my watch. Jillian wasn't due back to her store for a while. Her next appointment, I knew, wasn't until one p.m. She and another lady were teaching some type of cake decorating class upstairs. Therefore, I had a few hours to kill.

I remembered driving by a quaint little bookstore several weeks ago that I wanted to visit.

Perhaps they had some books about Egypt. What were the chances that I could find some information about mummies—and the curses involved should one reawaken—in a small town like this?

All I had to do was find the flippin' place. I had thought it was close to Jillian's shop. Clearly my memory and sense of direction were just as horrible as ever.

Ten minutes later I found it, after I finally remembered the picturesque store wasn't on Main, but off of Oregon Street. Turns out, it was less than two blocks from Cookbook Nook. I parked the Jeep, patted both corgis on the head, and stepped out into the fresh cool morning air. I heard the creak of a wooden sign swinging in the breeze and automatically looked up. I was looking at a hand-painted sign. A Lazy Afternoon. What a perfect name for a book store.

The store had a weathered brick façade, a large bay window, and a huge green awning stretching out over the entire width of the store. A whiskey barrel full of fragrant yellow petunias was sitting next to the door. I caught sight of the store hours as I pushed the door open. 9 a.m. to 2 p.m. Tuesday through Saturday.

A bell dinged loudly, announcing my presence. I glanced up, expecting to see a small brass bell mounted just inside the door like I've seen in countless other stores. Nothing. I then glanced down, expecting to see infrared sensors throwing an invisible beam across the entry. Nothing there, either. Shrugging, I moved deep into the heart of the store. I could hear the twang of a modern country song coming from somewhere close by and I instinctively headed toward it.

Then I heard the chime of the bell again. I glanced back at the door to see who else might have come in. Much to my surprise, I noticed the door was still closed and no one was there. Confused, still staring at the closed door, I heard the chime again. And again. I stared around the store in confusion. Someone had to be playing a trick on me.

"Don't worry about Ruby. She's been foolin' people for years."

I turned at the sound of the voice. A short elderly woman had appeared between two racks of books. I guessed her age to be late fifties to early sixties, although to be fair, I will admit that I sucked at guessing ages. She was as skinny as a rail, had inch-long fake nails (painted glittery red), and was wearing an outfit I usually saw on the younger crowd. The much younger crowd. Skin-tight jeans adorned with rhinestones and a button down light blue blouse showing way more than I needed to see. I got the impression this woman was trying—futilely—to reclaim her youth. I also had to refrain from whipping out my sunglasses. This woman had to have the brightest, palest, biggest mop of hair that I have ever seen on anyone. I managed to catch myself before I started to stare. Was it a wig? Hair that color, in that volume, couldn't possibly be natural.

"I'm Clara Hanson. Who might you be, sweetie?"

"Uh, Zack Anderson."

"Ah! So you're the guy I've heard so much about. Why'd it take you so long to stop by and introduce yourself?"

"Uh..."

"Oh, honey. All the store owners know everything about you. We know you were set up when you first moved to town. Why would anyone want to frame a handsome young thing like you, anyway?"

My sense of self-preservation kicked in and I took a few cautious steps back. Clara's arm instantly snaked out and hooked itself through mine, pulling me uncomfortably close to her. She leered up at me and smiled, displaying a mouth full of stained teeth. There's yet another reason why I'll never drink coffee.

"Oh, relax, darlin'. You have nothing to worry about. I don't bite. At least, not yet."

My eyes shot open. Holy crap on a cracker. I could feel my face flaming up. I had to get away from this woman.

"We all know you were set up," Clara continued, pulling me deeper into her store. Thankfully she hadn't noticed my face yet. "I knew there was no way you could be guilty of murder."

"How?" I asked, genuinely curious. "You don't even know me."

"True," Clara nodded, sending ripples up through her hair.

I was briefly reminded of someone dropping a rock in a pond and watching the ripples make their way across the surface. Her hair teetered precariously, convincing me I was looking at the most elaborate wig I had ever seen. However, the hair defied the call of gravity and stayed in place.

"It's a hunch, sweetie," Clara told me as she guided me over to a small counter complete with an old-fashioned push button cash register that belonged back in the '50s. "I'm a wonderful judge of character."

Yeah, I bet you are, lady. If I didn't hurry up and ask her where to find books on Egypt, then I had the distinct impression this woman would talk my ear off. I cleared my throat, but before I could say anything Clara's mouth was off and running.

"Ever since I lost my Leroy a few years ago to cancer," Clara said, as she led me away from the counter to give me an uncomfortably slow tour of her store, "I've decided to change my life. I've cut out sugars, carbs, and caffeine from my diet and replaced them with organic fruits and nuts."

I grunted as way of acknowledgement. Somehow this didn't surprise me.

"I've never felt better. I've never looked better, not even when I was forty years younger. I..."

"Do you have any books on Egypt?" I quickly asked as Clara paused to take a breath. "Pyramids, pharaohs, er, mummies. You know. I'm looking for that kind of thing."

Clara threw back her head and laughed. "Honey, you and everyone else! Ever since that mummy made off with King Tut's necklace last night, I've had a run on anything having to do with Egypt. I've already contacted my distributor and talked them into overnighting me another selection of books. I can't keep them on the shelf!"

My hopes fell.

"Oh. You're completely out? That stinks."

Clara sidled close and nudged me with her shoulder.

"Oh, honey, now don't you fret. I may have something left that would interest you."

The store owner finally released my arm and moved off through her racks of books, still chatting amicably away. It was right about then, when we passed by the far southwestern corner of the shop, that I discovered the source of the door chime. There was a vintage round, black, wrought iron bird cage sitting in the corner. The front door was open and sitting on a padded perch attached to the front of the cage was an African gray parrot. Clara noticed me staring at the bird and chuckled.

"Where are my manners? Zack, this is Ruby. Ruby, this is Zack, momma's newest friend."

"Give us a kiss, Precious," Ruby crooned, bobbing her head up and down as parrots were accustomed to doing. "Give us a kiss!"

I had to smile.

"So this is your security system. I have to hand

it to you. She sounded just like a bell."

"My security system consists of one camera, aimed at the door." Clara pointed at a small monitor sitting on a shelf just below the counter top. "Ruby can see it from her perch and has picked up the habit of chiming like a bell whenever she sees someone come in. The funny thing is, I never trained her to do it."

A cell phone rang loudly nearby. Both Clara and I reached for our respective cells at the same time. It wasn't mine. I looked over at Clara in time to see her glare at the bird.

"Ruby, I told you to stop doing that. It stopped being funny several weeks ago."

"Give us a kiss, give us a kiss."

I chuckled. "I take it Ruby is great at mimicking sounds she hears, huh?"

"This latest one is a real pain," Clara admitted with a sigh. "Ruby has unfortunately learned that it's great fun to make a certain noise and watch me scramble like a mad woman for my cell. I've threatened to withhold snacks. I've tried to bribe her with her favorite treats. Nothing works. I can only hope this is just a rebellious phase."

"How old is she?" I asked, looking at the small gray parrot.

"Twenty-five."

"Really? How long do parrots live?"

"Ruby will be around long after I'm gone," Clara said. "Healthy greys can live up to eighty years on a balanced diet."

"Wow. It's crazy to think she could live for another 55 years!"

"I've raised her from a chick," Clara told me. "I give her only the best organic, balanced food. She sees Dr. Watt several times a year to get her talons and her beak trimmed. She's a healthy little thing. I just worry about what'll happen to her once I'm gone."

Was I being set up? The hairs on the back of my neck were standing straight up.

"I'm sure you have a long way to go before that happens," I tried to assure her.

"Let's hope so," Clara agreed, giving me a strained smile. "Now, then. It just so happens that I have one copy left of Egyptian Mummies and Their Curses for Idiots book."

"You can't be serious," I stammered. "There's a book about Egyptian curses in that series? And you had more than one copy?"

"I had six," Clara confessed.

"That's…" I trailed off as the implication set in.

"Presumptuous?" Clara offered. "Look, Zack, I know how it looks. I can only assure you that I had nothing to do with what happened last night. What I can tell you is that I had people waiting on my doorstep before I even got here this morning. They were waiting to buy books about Egypt and mummies in particular. I'm selling you the copy I had reserved for myself."

"Oh. Hey, I can't take your book. You take it."

"I'll have a dozen more in a few days," Clara confided. She shook her head, causing her full head of hair to dip dangerously low. I was still waiting for the wig to come tumbling off. "You take this one. I can wait."

"Why were there so many people waiting to buy books about Egypt?" I asked, perplexed, as I handed my credit card to Clara. There were clearly plenty of freaked out people, like me, doing a little more, er, investigative research.

Clara paused just before swiping my card through the credit card machine. The look on her face was not something I was expecting. Her eyebrows shot up and her eyes opened wide.

"You mean you don't know about last night?"

"I was there last night," I huffed, growing defensive. "I know full well what happened during the presentation."

"I'm not talking about what happened at the school," Clara said, dropping her voice to a whisper, "but rather what happened on D Street. This would have been after the event broke up last night."

"What about D Street?" I wanted to know, curious. "Did something happen?"

"Someone saw the mummy!" Clara excitedly told me, keeping her voice low. "It was shuffling along D Street and disappeared into the nearby trees before the police could arrive."

I felt the blood drain from my face. No. It simply couldn't be. Mummies do not rise from the dead. They simply cannot be reanimated. I was joking earlier. I swear! I seriously had to stop watching so many movies.

"That's impossible," I assured Clara, adopting the strongest, most confident voice I could muster. "Mummies can't come back to life."

"This one did!" Clara assured me. "Five different people saw it! It happened just after midnight."

Even though I'm sure my heart was pounding, a nagging thought occurred, which caused me to frown. There had been witnesses? At that time of night?

"What were that many people doing awake in the middle of the night?" I skeptically asked.

Clara's brow furrowed. I could tell she hadn't been expecting that question. She looked at me and chuckled.

"That's a mighty fine question, Zack. I don't have an answer for you. I can only relay what I've heard. Everyone is spooked. Everyone wants to know what we're dealing with. As a result, people are buying up whatever they can find about mummies."

Clara placed my newly purchased book into a white paper bag with handles and slid it across the counter to me.

"There you are. If you find anything interesting in there you be sure to let me know!"

"You got it. Nice meeting you, Clara."

"And you, sweetie. Don't be a stranger next time. Come back soon!"

I exited the store and hurried to my Jeep. I had the distinct feeling that if I didn't get out of there, and quickly, then Clara was going to somehow get me back inside her store.

Before you get the wrong impression, I should tell you that no, I'm not afraid of little old ladies. However, with that being said, I need to tell you that I am not a fan of people who don't respect your personal space. We can still carry on a conversation and not have to be less than six inches apart from one another, thank you very much.

As I merged onto Oregon and turned onto Main Street, I thought back to what Clara had said. There had been mummy sightings. Wouldn't that suggest ... no. Nope. We're not going there. It's not possible. Period. I needed to do something to get my mind off of things.

I made a decision about what I wanted to do and started heading back home, intent on dropping the dogs off at the house for a few hours. I hit the "Hands Free" icon on my stereo and was rewarded with a synthetic female voice asking what I wanted to do.

"Call Vance."

"How can I be of service today?" my stereo asked again, using its flat, featureless monotone.

"Call Vance," I crossly repeated.

"What type of dance would you like me to research online?"

"Vance, you moron. Call Vance. Now."

"Searching."

"Searching?" I repeated. "Come on, you idiotic hunk of junk. I only have one Vance in my phonebook. He's not hard to find."

"I found one dance studio less than three miles from your present location," my smart phone informed me. "Would you like directions?"

With an irritated huff, I disconnected my oh-so-wonderful hands free assistant and fished the phone out of my pocket. Yes, I already know you're not supposed to mess with your phone while you're in the car. Especially when you're driving. However, it was either that or else I'd end up flipping off the stereo and it'd be my luck someone I knew would see me do it.

"Yo, Zack. What's up?"

"Hey, Vance. Are you still interested in catching a movie today? I need to do something to take my mind off of things."

"Would that have anything to do with the events of last night?"

"Don't start with me," I crossly muttered. "Yes or no."

"Sorry, buddy. I'll have to take a rain check."

"Oh, come on," I complained. "Rambo: Old Blood looks pretty good! They say Sylvester Stallone promised to do all his own stunts this time!"

"There's no way, pal. When you have that much money you don't take a chance of getting hurt. Listen. Forget about that for now. Are you bored? Need something to do? Get yourself over to Fanny's Farms. And bring the dogs."

"What? What for?"

"You're not gonna like it if I tell you."

"Just tell me it has nothing to do with last night."

"Sorry, pal. There's been a mummy sighting. It was witnessed by nearly a dozen people."

"Yeah, I know. Clara at the bookstore told me all about it. I guess it happened sometime after midnight. I thought it was off of D Street and not at some farm."

"It was off of some farm. And you're right. That happened last night. I already know all about it. The one I'm referring to happened less than an hour ago, Zack."

"Oh, no."

"Come on, pal. Pull it together. You know someone is pranking us. There's no way this is legit. Look. Think of it as therapy, okay?"

"I knew I should have never told you about my preference to avoid anything having to do with mummies."

"You didn't. I guessed, remember? You just confirmed my suspicions. Right now, in fact."

I groaned again.

"It'll do you good. Will you do it?"

"You actually want me out at a crime scene?"

"If you bring the dogs, yes."

"And if I don't?"

"Well…"

"Thanks a lot, pal. Fine. You win."

"Great! I'll see you there!"

"I swear, man, if I so much as see a..."

The phone beeped and the call was over. I sighed. Swell. There was another sighting? In broad daylight? What the heck was going on around here, anyway? Was Vance right? Was this just some elaborate hoax? Or was I right and the mummy had...

I shuddered, even before I could finish the thought. Vance was right. I needed to deal with this irrational fear of mine. There was no way that a mummy had come back to life. Nope. No, sir. Nuh-uh.

Maybe if I say it enough times then I'll actually start to believe it.

Fanny's Farms was probably the second largest farm to participate in Cider Fest. They, like Greenwood Gardens, had to resort to parking visiting cars wherever there was room. In this case, since Fanny's Farms was more wooded than the last farm I had been to, I had to park my Jeep directly between two trees. I barely had enough room to open the doors.

I could smell fresh pine, which wasn't surprising since there were pine trees everywhere. There was also a layer of pine needles coating the ground, with an occasional pine cone thrown in here and there. I set their royal majesties down on the ground, clipped leashes onto both of them, and headed in the same direction that everyone else seemed to be going.

Looks like the big draw of this farm, according to the numerous signs I was passing, was a huge 40-acre corn maze. According to the sign I just passed, the quickest reported time in which the maze had been solved had been just under an hour. Management recommended, according to the sign, that you purchase a whistle before you enter. The corn stalks were easily over eight feet tall and grew incredibly thick. It was quite easy to become lost and grow frustrated. Therefore, three blasts on the whistle would alert the staff and you'd be rescued. Much to the amusement of your friends, I'm sure.

Sherlock led me straight to the entrance of the maze, where Vance was waiting for me. Two other police officers were there, preventing people from entering the maze.

"Hey, Zack. Glad you could make it."

"Yeah, right," I snorted. I looked down at the dogs, who were both presently staring at Vance. "You're just happy to see them."

Vance squatted, reached into a jacket pocket, and produced two dog biscuits. Two corgi butts immediately plunked down on the ground. He held out both biscuits to the dogs, who took them so gently I was convinced they'd be able to hold a soap bubble in their jaws without breaking it.

"You little snots," I said, looking disdainfully down at the dogs. "You nearly bite my fingers off whenever I give you treats. Why are you giving him the preferential treatment?"

"Maybe they like me better?" Vance casually suggested as he stood back up.

"Bite me."

"Case closed, pal."

"Mm-hmm. Are you going to tell me what's going on? Why are we here? And why are we at the maze?"

Vance turned and disappeared through the entrance of the maze, visible only as an opening cut into a huge eight-foot-tall wall of corn.

"Come on," Vance called. "Follow me. There's something you need to see."

"You want me to go in there?"

Vance shot me a look over his shoulder as he pushed by several swaying stalks of corn.

"Is that a problem? Don't tell me you're claustrophobic, too."

"Bite me, pal. I'm referring to that sign back there that says it takes close to an hour to solve this thing. Sounds to me like it's easy to get lost in there. Do you know where we need to go?"

Vance's only response was to hold up a folded piece of paper. I could tell something was printed on it but I couldn't make it out. He held it out behind him, forcing me to increase my pace if I wanted to see what was on it.

"What's that?" I asked.

"Cheat sheet."

"To what? The maze? Seriously?"

"You didn't think I'd come in here without knowing how to get out, right?"

I took the paper and glanced down at it. What I saw had me groaning out loud. I was looking at an overview of what the maze must look like from a bird's eye view. These people definitely had way too much time on their hands.

I was looking at a map of the continental United States of America. However, someone had cleverly turned the USA map into a maze. It looked as though the entrance to the maze was located in the southern tip of Texas while the finish line was the Olympic Peninsula in Washington State. As mazes go, it didn't look too complex. However, I'm pretty sure most mazes weren't created on a 40-acre field of corn. It was gonna take time to make it through that sucker. My feet ached at the prospect.

"Are you kidding me?" I groaned.

"Fanny's Farms is serious about their corn mazes," Vance explained, leading me deeper into the corn. "I think they've won awards for it."

"Really? They give out awards for mazes?"

"It's just to get into the spirit of things. Damn, Zack. Why so negative? Don't people in the big city celebrate the holidays?"

"Sorry," I apologized. "This small town atmosphere still takes some getting used to. So where are we going?"

"I was told we need to head to Michigan."

I looked down at the maze's overlay and tapped an area in the northeast.

"That'd be over here somewhere. Are you sure we can find it?"

Vance took back the map.

"Of course we can. We can do this."

"We need to get to Michigan? Couldn't we just drive over there and save ourselves the trouble of navigating through that?"

"Drive over where?" Vance asked, looking back at me. "Do you see any roads around here? This whole area is nothing but corn. The Martinsons have nearly two hundred acres of it. That doesn't even include the other crops they grow."

"Oh."

"Are you done complaining? Now follow me."

"Lead the way pal. Just don't get us lost."

"Please," Vance scoffed. "I'm a detective. There's no way."

Fifteen minutes of endless wandering finally convinced Vance to concede defeat. He had gotten us lost. I noticed he was wearing a whistle and I also noticed he had eyed it more than once. As soon as he stopped to stare at the map for the tenth time since arriving in this Hee Haw Hell, I quickly approached and tapped the cheap plastic toy dangling around his neck.

"Maybe we should…"

Vance slapped my hand away.

"Hell no. I'd never live it down. Neither would you."

"Everyone knows I have a lousy sense of direction," I explained. "It's expected of me. It's nice to see it happen to someone besides me."

Vance looked down at Sherlock.

"What do you say, buddy? Care to help me out?"

Sherlock, thus far content to simply explore the corn field with us, lifted his head and sniffed. Watson continued to stare at Vance, hoping he'd offer her another biscuit. Sherlock tugged at his leash and led us back the way we had come. I looked over at Vance, who shrugged and held out a hand, indicating we should lead the way.

For ten minutes Sherlock wove his way through the stalks of corn, not once bothering to see if we were all following. I took off my jacket and slung it over my shoulder. The temperature inside the corn field was sweltering. It had to be at least twenty degrees warmer than the outside air, making the ambient temp somewhere around the mid-80s. I could feel beads of sweat trickling down my back.

I glanced down at the dogs and noted their thick coats. This couldn't be pleasant for them. I certainly wouldn't want to be traipsing around a corn field wearing a fur coat. But, as I watched Sherlock sniffing along the row of corn, I could see that he didn't appear to be distressed in the slightest. Nor did Watson. On the contrary, both corgis appeared to be having the times of their lives.

Just then we passed a family of five, being led in the opposite direction by a young girl in coveralls. Ordinarily I'd chalk that up to poor fashion sense. However, I had seen other kids wearing the same getup when I had parked my Jeep, so I had to assume that was what Fanny's Farms was making their employees wear. Poor saps. Working on a farm and being forced to wear that hillbilly getup? They had my deepest sympathies.

"But why do we hafta leave?" I heard one of the small children ask. I glanced back to see the father reach down to scoop up his young daughter.

"The police said we have to," the father patiently explained. "They need to check things out to make sure it's safe, honey."

"I heard that it was only hanging on by a thread!" a ten-year-old boy added.

"What was hanging on by a thread?" I heard the mother ask.

I noticed Vance had stopped to listen, too. Both corgis felt their leashes go taut and gave us exasperated looks. Sherlock tugged on his leash. He wanted to keep going.

"The mummy's head, of course," the boy proudly answered. "I heard the head was flopping around so much that people thought it was gonna fall off!"

"Eww!" the young girl exclaimed, burying her head in her father's chest.

"Charlie, you heard no such thing," the mother

scolded.

"Did so!" Charlie whined.

"Did not," the father added, with a wink. "They did say that the mummy was seen dragging its leg, holding its arms outstretched, and rasping on about getting his hands on five-year-old girls. Hmm, if only I knew of some."

"Dadddddy!" the girl shrieked, as predicted.

"You'll know the mummy is near when you hear its piteous moans," the father added, winking at his sons.

Charlie proceeded to add the appropriate sound effects as the family moved off. I could hear the little girl's shrieks long after I had lost sight of them. I turned to Vance and shook my head.

"Stories like those are going to blow this out of proportion."

"All the more reason to nip this in the bud while we still can," Vance agreed.

"Why would a mummy want to come to a corn field?" I asked just as we were moving again. "It doesn't make sense."

Vance shook his head. "The more appropriate question would be, why would a person steal a mummy and then make it look like the mummy visited a corn maze?"

"Still think someone is pranking us?" I asked.

"Still think the mummy came back to life on its own?" Vance countered. "Of the two of us, which one sounds improbable?"

We arrived in 'Michigan' a few minutes later. I

don't know how Sherlock knew where we needed to go. Perhaps he followed a number of scent trails there? However he did it, I'm glad he did. If it had been up to the humans then we'd still be lost somewhere around Georgia, I'm sure.

We came upon a junction of at least five different paths and found a group of 'uniformed' kids blocking access from each direction. Were we the first on the scene? From an incident that happened over an hour ago? I glanced over at Vance to see him frowning at the kids.

"Would've thought there'd be more people here," I softly muttered.

"That makes two of us," Vance agreed. He singled out the closest staff member, a boy of about sixteen, and motioned him over. "Detective Vance Samuelson. How long have you kids been securing this location?"

"Umm, about twenty minutes," the boy shyly answered. "Uh, sir."

"And yet this 'sighting'," Vance continued, throwing in some air quotes, "happened over an hour ago! Why wasn't it reported sooner?"

"I dunno. We were busy?"

Vance took a couple of deep, calming breaths. He dismissed the boy and began studying the ground. Sherlock sniffed at a set of footprints, looked back at Watson to see what she was looking at, and then began canvassing the area in ever-widening loops. I heard several of the kids comment on how cute the dogs looked.

"So what do you see?" I asked Vance as I saw him squat down on the exposed dirt in the path.

The detective pointed at several scuffs in the dirt.

"Do you see here? This groove? It looks like someone was dragging something."

"Like someone was dragging a leg?" I nonchalantly asked. "A dead, lifeless leg?"

"Would you forget about that for a moment? Look at this." Vance tapped a nondescript scuff in the dirt. "This is odd."

"What is it?" I asked.

"It looks like whoever left this print suffered an injury. This is a print from someone's right foot. See this? This was made by a broken toe."

"A mummy could have a broken toe."

"I knew I shouldn't have told you," Vance grumbled, straightening up. "You need to ... where are they going?"

I felt a tug on a leash. Sherlock apparently didn't think there was anything more to learn by staring at the dirt and was leading us away. We were angling toward a path guarded by a pimply-faced teen boy. The teen's eyes widened with surprise as he noticed our approach.

"Step aside, son," Vance ordered.

"Umm, I'm not supposed to..."

"Step. Aside. Now."

The boy moved out of the way just as Sherlock pushed by him. We were led about twenty feet down the path when the corgi stopped. He looked back over his shoulder and watched us approach. Sherlock then dropped his gaze to Watson and stepped to the side just as she arrived. He nosed a few stalks then turned back, as if checking to see if Watson had noticed the same thing he had.

"What is it, boy?" Vance asked as he squatted down next to Sherlock. "What do you ... is that a ...? Holy cow!"

"What?" I demanded, hurrying over to Vance's side. "What have you ... no way. Tell me that's not what I think it is."

It was. Several feet inside the corn I could see a form lying face down on the ground, arms and legs bent and twisted into unnatural positions. It was a body, wearing torn khaki trousers, a dark green long sleeve shirt, and thick soled work boots. I hurriedly looked over at Vance. I had seen that outfit before. We both had. Dr. Tarik's staff members had been wearing this uniform when they rushed up on the stage after learning the pendant had been stolen.

"Help me roll him over," Vance instructed. "We need to check for a pulse. Hurry!"

As soon as I laid a hand on the still form's shoulder, I knew we were wasting our time. And I was right. What we found sent chills down my spine and will probably haunt my dreams for quite some time.

The body had been mummified.

FOUR

W hat do you think?" Vance asked quietly as he studied the shriveled flesh, the sunken eyes, and the mouth stuck open in a never-ending scream of terror.

"You don't want to know what I think," I told him, straightening up and pulling the dogs away from the body. "You can't sit there and tell me that the mummy didn't do this."

"There's just no way," Vance murmured, as he slowly stood up. "Did you notice the clothes?"

I nodded. "Yep. Dr. Tarik's assistants were wearing that outfit when they rushed on stage. Which one do you think it is?"

"There's no proof it's any of them," Vance hastily pointed out. "Don't jump to conclusions, Zack."

"But..."

"No matter how compelling the evidence," Vance hastily added.

"There's an awful lot of evidence pointing squarely at that mummy," I reminded my detective friend.

"True," Vance admitted, "but you and I both know there must be some other explanation. We just have to find it."

"Where do we start?" I pointedly asked. "And are we even allowed to get involved? This is a police matter."

Vance pulled his cell from his pocket and stared hard at me.

"As soon as I make this call, then PV is gonna go ape. This place is going to be overrun by anyone and everyone with a scanner. Cops, techs, reporters, video crews, goofs who think they're mummy hunters, etcetera. As much as I hate to say it, this sort of thing will probably make the nightly news all the way up in Portland."

I nodded. "Okay. What does that have to do with me?"

"I need to tell you something. You have no idea what this case is doing to Tori."

I was silent as I thought about it. I could only imagine what she was going through. From the sounds of it, it had been Tori's insistence that Egyptian Exhibitions had even stopped in PV. That had to make her look guilty in everyone's eyes. Even Dr. Tarik had insinuated she was involved on the night of the theft.

"Come on, Zack. Help me out here. She may not show it, but I can see this is totally stressing her out. I don't like to see her like this."

"You're putting a lot of faith in Sherlock," I quietly said, dropping my voice so that the kids standing guard nearby couldn't overhear. "What makes you so sure he can help?"

"You told me how much Sherlock helped you when we all thought you were guilty of murder," Vance reminded me. "Myself, included. He found the painting with the blood on it. He found that old picture of Bonnie Davies and her family. He even found the missing glass tiger. I'm willing to accept his help if he's willing to give it."

Sherlock sidled up to Vance and whined. The detective scratched behind his ears and slipped him another biscuit. In less time than it takes to ask if Watson was interested, she appeared next to Sherlock and dutifully sat next to him. Once both corgis had finished their treats, I gathered up the leashes and gave them a gentle tug.

"Well, I'll see if he can find anything. You find out what the mummy was doing out here."

"There's still no proof the mummy is alive," Vance insisted. "I … no, stop pointing at the body, Zack. There's gotta be some other explanation. Now, go with the dogs. See what they can find. I'll take care of things here."

"Fine. Give me the whistle."

Vance passed over the cheap plastic signal. After a moment's hesitation he held out the map.

"You'd better take this, too."

"Smartass."

I tucked the map and whistle into a pocket and looked down at the dogs. Sherlock looked up at me, waiting to see what I was going to do. I looked back at the body in time to see Vance pull out his cell.

"Okay, you two. Do your thing."

Sherlock stared at me and cocked his head. Watson promptly sat. Sherlock must've decided it was a good idea so he sat, too.

"What are you doing? Come on, guys. He gave you treats. Get up and get going."

Acting as though he had forgotten he had just been given a retainer for the case, Sherlock got to his feet, sniffed once at the body, and then moved off, heading back out of the maze, toward the east coast if I remembered the map correctly. I felt a tap on my shoulder. Vance was on the phone and was holding up a finger, indicating I should wait. A few minutes later he finished his call and approached.

"Where are you going? Shouldn't they check out the body to see if there's anything they missed?"

I indicated Sherlock.

"He already looked. I watched him do it. Apparently, he feels there isn't anything else to be learned here. In fact, he wants to go that way."

Vance turned to look east. There was nothing but swaying corn stalks as far as the eye could see, which wasn't far considering the darn things were taller than we were. The detective looked down at Sherlock and shrugged.

"Fine. You guys go that way. If you find anything, give three blasts on the whistle."

I waggled my cell in front of him.

"Or I could just call you?"

Vance shrugged. "Whatever."

"Are you sure we shouldn't wait for you?" I asked, growing concerned. I still wasn't convinced a 3,000-year-old dead dude wasn't walking around out there.

"I've already made the call. Backup is going to be here in less than fifteen minutes. If you guys are going to find anything then you need to get going. Now."

"Got it. Sherlock, lead the way."

We followed a trail that, according to the map, led us from Michigan, through Ohio, across Pennsylvania, and then up to the northern reaches of New York. That was where we encountered the northern border of the corn maze and, consequently, a tiny dirt road that was barely wide enough to pass a small car. That was also where Sherlock lost the trail.

I phoned Vance and informed him of what we had found.

"I knew it. I knew there wasn't any mummy involved. Whoever dumped the body must've had a car waiting for them. Then they simply drove off."

"No one said they heard any cars," I pointed out. "It's awful quiet out here. You think someone would have noticed if they heard a car driving away. And didn't you say there weren't any roads out here?"

"A valid point," Vance admitted with a sigh.

"And what about that mummified person?" I asked, leading the dogs back into the maze and heading west toward the exit. "You can't tell me it's a coincidence that we suspect a mummy has stolen a pendant and then an actual mummified person appears in a corn field? What are the odds of that happening?"

"We don't suspect a mummy," Vance corrected. "You do."

"You know what I mean. Do we have any idea who the new mummy is?"

"I've called for Dr. Tarik. I don't know if he'd be able to identify the body by facial recognition alone. The features are all severely distorted. I can only assume he can tell us if his staff is all accounted for. If he can't, well, then we'll know."

"What do you want me to do now? We found a road where none was supposed to exist. Sherlock hasn't given any indication he wants to look at anything else out here. With that being said, I'm presently heading for the exit. I don't think you'd want me or the dogs hanging around there."

"Good thinking. Tell you what. Go home, Zack. If it's okay with you, I'll swing by after I'm done here. Then we can compare notes."

"Sounds like a plan. I'll see you back at the house."

The house I had inherited was a large two-story country farmhouse located on a 40-acre plot of land southeast of town. As I mentioned earlier, I had also inherited a winery. Lentari Cellars, I had been surprised to learn, was a local favorite. In fact, people were known to horde those slender green bottles with the ancient parchment labels. I had thrown a grand re-opening of the winery last month and made presents of most of the existing supply of stock I found in the back storeroom. It was a fantastic way to make new friends and to prove to everyone that I wasn't a cold-blooded killer after all. And yes, for once I'm not being facetious.

Caden, my self-appointed wine master, had the vines trimmed, fertilized, and even replanted when some of the existing vines were discovered dead. He had all the machinery in the winery professionally cleaned, serviced, and running in top form. In fact, our first harvest was due to happen in the next week or so. I had reluctantly agreed to share the first bottle that came off the line with him, regardless of type or flavor. And yes, Vance had begged to be included. I'm sure he just wants to witness me trying to choke down a glass of wine.

Jerk.

Whatever. The acres of vines were looking good. Our first harvest was almost already sold out, all without us producing a single bottle. I had two dogs that meant the world to me, accompanying me practically everywhere I go. Life was good.

Or at least it had been until that mummy came back to life. Yeah, I know what you're thinking.

I'm being a fool. Only children believed mummies could find some way to become reanimated. Well, I'd like to see how fast you'd change your mind if you were to discover a, let me see if I remember the proper word, desiccated human corpse in a field of corn. You can't possibly tell me that it wouldn't cross your mind that somehow the mummy might be involved.

Vance phoned nearly two hours later to say he had just left the station. Since it was past 5 p.m. I could only assume Vance, like myself, hadn't eaten. I ordered pizzas and waited for my detective friend to arrive. When he finally did pull into the driveway, I had the beers ready. However, I was surprised to see that he wasn't alone. Tori was with him.

Uh-oh. Was I supposed to have called Jillian over? I ducked back inside and hurriedly phoned her.

"Zack! What a pleasant surprise!"

"Hi, Jillian. Listen, do you have any plans for tonight?"

"As a matter of fact, I do."

My hopes fell. If Vance had Tori with him, then I would have really liked to have had Jillian here. It's not that I'm afraid to be in the house with another woman, especially if she's the wife of my friend, but there's something about a single guy trying to hang out with a married couple. All you single people out there should be able to back me up. No one likes to feel like a third wheel.

"Oh. I'm sorry. I was hoping I could encourage you to come over."

"Oh? Why's that? Is it because Vance and Tori are currently on their way over?"

Uh, oh. This didn't bode well.

"Umm, how did you know that? Did Tori tell you?"

"As a matter of fact, she did. Look, Zack, if you're busy tonight, it's okay. You just have to tell me."

I was definitely missing something here.

"I'm not sure I follow."

"We talked about this. Yesterday. We were planning on watching a movie tonight. Remember when you told me that you and Samantha used to watch movies together on Friday nights? Well, I offered to keep the tradition going. In her memory. You said that you were okay with it at the time. If it's bringing up too many painful memories, then I understand. We can try again some other night."

"Movie night?" I repeated, feeling stupid.

I heard Jillian start to laugh into the phone. I had to wait a full twenty seconds before she was able to compose herself. She cleared her throat, waited a few more seconds, and then started talking again.

"Now it makes sense."

"What does?" I asked, bewildered.

"You forgot. You forgot about our plans tonight, even when I set a reminder on your phone."

I pulled my cell out of my pocket and stared at it.

"What about my phone?"

"Has it been making any noise?" Jillian casually asked.

"Not that I can recall."

"What about a series of beeps? Maybe every five minutes or so?"

Come to think of it, I did remember hearing something beeping. I had assumed it was coming from somewhere else, like maybe a smoke detector? I tapped the screen on my smart phone and sure enough, a big angry message appeared. It was a reminder to pick Jillian up at 5 p.m.

I looked at the clock. 5:05 p.m. Well, rats.

"How about that."

"So you're okay with me coming over? I was afraid that I had been pushing too hard."

"I'm totally fine with you coming over," I assured her. "Although I will probably have to take a rain check on the movie. I think Vance wants to go over the case."

"Oh, about the missing pendant? That's okay. I'll agree to a rain check if I get to pick the movie."

"That's fine, Jillian."

"Any movie."

"Wait, what?"

"Any movie. My choice. You have to sit and watch it with me without any electronic devices in the room. No cell, no tablet, no internet, no nothing. Agreed?"

"You drive a hard bargain," I groaned. "Fine. You win. I agree."

"Excellent! When would you like me to come over?"

I heard the slams of car doors coming from outside. Vance and Tori were walking up the porch steps. I sighed.

"How about now? And if you're asked, no mentioning I forgot to pick you up. Deal?"

Jillian laughed again.

"It's a deal, Zachary."

An hour later, after we had polished off most of the pizza and I had put the leftovers into the fridge, we retired to the living room. Jillian and I angled for the couch, but Vance and Tori beat us there. Vance grinned at me as Jillian and I were forced to sit on the loveseat.

For the record, both Sherlock and Watson were hanging out next to Vance.

"So what did the crime scene techs find out about the body?" I eagerly asked. "Could you tell who it was?"

"You saw the condition of it," Vance said, after taking a long swig from his beer. "It's going to be some time before any attempts at a positive identification can be made."

"I just can't believe this is happening," Tori said again, holding her head in her hands. "I can't believe that this happened to them in our small town. Why couldn't this have waited until they were in Portland?"

"I'm just sorry that pendant was stolen," Jillian added, taking a sip from her own beer. "It's probably long gone from here by now."

Vance held up a hand, "On the contrary, we think the pendant is still here in PV."

"You do?" I asked, surprised.

"You do?" Tori echoed. "Why?"

Vance leaned forward to set his beer on the coffee table. Tori frowned and pointed at a coaster. Vance sighed, picked up his bottle, and slid a coaster under it.

"Think about it. PV is a small town. Any outsider would've been noticed immediately. We've called in every off-duty officer we have and even borrowed a dozen from Medford. There are so many cops in PV now that you can't spit on the sidewalk without getting a citation."

"What are you saying?" I asked.

"This is the work of someone local," Vance answered, reaching for his beer.

"But who knew about the pendant's history?" I asked, confused. "Don't you remember what Dr. Tarik said? Only he knew that the pendant was real and authentic. He hadn't even told his personal assistant its true nature. Hey, speaking of the good doctor, did he say if he knew who the victim was? Could he account for all of his staff?"

Vance polished off the beer and set the bottle back on the table.

"All but one."

"The assistant," I guessed. "The one who

showed us the picture of the pendant in the book, is that right?"

"Ammar," Vance agreed. "He hasn't checked out of the hotel yet, and his bed hasn't been touched. It means he never made it back to the hotel after we saw him the night of the heist."

"The mummy got him," I decided, knowing full well that it would get a rise out of everyone present.

"Don't start with the mummy again," Vance complained. "This isn't a movie, alright? There isn't some curse at play here, nor is there any plot to have the mummy take over the world. Let it go, buddy."

Tori suddenly frowned. "Wait a moment. There's no way the victim is Ammar. Mummification takes a long time. It's not an overnight process. It can take upwards of three months for a body to become completely dried out."

"Desiccated," I supplied, showing off my newfound word of the day.

Jillian beamed a smile and patted my knee.

"It's so cute when you try."

"So who did know about the pendant's true history?" Tori asked. "Besides me, that is."

"What?" Vance sputtered, turning to look at his wife. "You knew?"

Tori nodded guiltily. "Yes. I figured it out. Egyptian Exhibitions maintains photographs of everything in their collection. They've actually made publicity pamphlets out of it. You can download and print it directly from their website, which I did. Now, you have to understand, I have an eidetic memory."

"Is that the technical term for 'photographic memory'?" I asked.

Tori shook her head. "No. Although it's close. Eidetic means I have extraordinarily accurate and vivid powers of recall. I can typically remember what I see."

"It's a pain," Vance sniggered. "I can never win an argument."

Tori swatted his arm.

"Now, as I was saying, as someone with an eidetic memory, I studied the publicity pamphlet and essentially memorized all the pieces in the collection. So imagine my surprise when, a few days before the exhibit opened, I was touring the auditorium with Dr. Tarik when I saw something that didn't match anything in the pamphlets."

"The pendant," Jillian breathed, amazed.

"Right. The pendant. Oh, don't get me wrong, the pendant was in the pamphlet, but not that exact version of it. The colors were off and the tip of one of the feathers was chipped when the photo in the pamphlet showed a vulture in pristine condition. I knew a switch had been made. I just didn't say anything to Dr. Tarik about it."

"There aren't many people who would have been able to do what you just did," Jillian told her. "That's impressive."

"A search on the internet confirmed my suspicions. It was the authentic Nekhbet Pendant, once owned by King Tut himself."

"Did you tell anyone this?" Vance demanded, incredulous. "Please tell me you didn't."

"Of course I didn't, you nitwit," Tori admonished. "I'm not stupid. I knew full well what would happen if word got out that a priceless Egyptian artifact happened to be in PV."

"And yet, look what happened," Vance reminded her. "We need to prove that someone else figured it out, too, or..." The detective trailed off.

"Or what?" Tori asked, dropping her voice down into the don't-even-go-there level every married man was familiar with.

"This makes you look guilty, Tor," Vance told her as gently as he could. "I know you didn't do it; everyone here knows you didn't do it, but if it ever became known that you knew of the pendant's history? It'll look bad. That's all I'm saying."

"Then you need to figure this out before that can happen," Tori calmly told her husband. "You're the detective. Let's hear what the PVPD has figured out so far."

Vance turned to me and then deliberately looked down at the snoozing corgis.

"I already said we'll help," I assured my friend. "As much as we can. Let's hear what you've got. Then we'll decide what to do later."

"What can you tell us about what's happened?" Jillian asked. "Do you have any leads?"

Vance shook his head. "No. Not yet. We thought

for certain the pendant was still in the high school. We searched every single person in that school before they were allowed to leave. No one had it. I'm sorry to say the pendant is still missing and we still don't have a suspect there. Now, either Zack is right and the mummy has it or else it has been very expertly hidden."

"So we don't know where the pendant is," Tori repeated, "and the police don't have any suspects. Where does that leave us?"

"I say we go take a look at the high school again," I suggested.

Vance glanced my way and waited for an explanation.

"Let's assume that what you say is true," I began. "The pendant wasn't on any of the people leaving the auditorium. We're pretty sure the heist was orchestrated by a local. I think maybe the pendant was stashed somewhere in the school. And if it was, who better to find it than Wonder Mutt and his sidekick?"

"You want to go to the school?" Jillian asked. "Now?"

"I'm sorry. This wasn't the night I had planned for us."

Tori leaned forward, interested.

"Oooo, do tell!"

Jillian blushed. I'm sure I did, too. Vance stared at his wife, horrified.

"Tor-i! That's none of our business!"

"That's so not what I meant," I hastily added. I

couldn't meet Jillian's eyes, although I did hear a giggle coming from her direction. "What I meant was, would you care to go on a little excursion with us?"

"To check out the school?" Jillian asked, wiping her eyes with a tissue she pulled from her purse.

"Yes. I know it's nowhere on the list of things you want to do tonight, but..."

"Of course I'll go," Jillian interrupted. "We're searching for clues, right? Count me in. It sounds fun!"

As we were all heading outside, toward our cars, Vance passed by me and whispered in my ear.

"This girl wants to go hunting for clues on a Friday night? At a school? Zack, you need to marry this girl."

"Shut your mouth," I hissed back.

Vance chuckled as he unlocked his door. Then he saw me holding the door open for Jillian and, not to be outdone, hurried around his car to hold the door open for Tori. I helped the dogs into the back of the Jeep and we were off.

"Thanks for coming along," I told Jillian. "I know this can't be anywhere on your fun-things-to-do-on-a-Friday-night list, but I am glad you're here."

Jillian took my hand in hers and gave it a gentle squeeze.

"It's okay. I don't mind. It's not often a girl can say she helped look for clues with a man and his dogs. I actually feel a bit like Daphne or Velma."

I snickered in response.

"Wouldn't that make you Freddie?" Jillian continued. She looked back at Sherlock and ruffled his ears. "And that'd make you Scooby, wouldn't it? You're such a pretty boy."

Sherlock's mouth fell open and he panted contentedly. Watson was curled up in her seat, hiding her nose under a paw. I hadn't noticed that behavior before. Was she cold? Was she in pain? Then it hit. Rotten broccoli.

"Oh, my," Jillian exclaimed, holding a hand over her nose. "Those sure are powerful, aren't they?"

I cursed silently and jabbed a finger down on the window controls. We needed a rapid venting and we needed it now. I'm surprised the windows hadn't melted.

"Are you sure she's okay?" Jillian asked, concerned. "That can't be good on her system."

"Harry is pretty sure she eats too fast," I explained. "It must have happened with her previous owner. He's guessing Watson must have thought it was the only way to be sure she would get her food, so she inhales it as fast as she can. I keep trying to slow her down but so far nothing has worked."

Before I knew it, we were walking through PVHS's halls once more. As before, the school was deathly quiet. Vance was leading us back to the auditorium when suddenly Sherlock threw on the brakes. His nose lifted and he sniffed the air. Watson joined him a few seconds later.

We were standing in the middle of a junction of corridors. The hall we had been walking down was lined with lockers. This second hallway also had lockers. It stretched off to the east for at least a hundred feet before terminating in an exterior perimeter door.

Sherlock tugged his leash. He wanted to go down the new corridor. I looked over at Vance, who shrugged. I gave Sherlock permission to go and started after him. Watson trotted along beside him, content to keep pace with him. Jillian was walking beside me with Vance and Tori bringing up the rear.

Just as suddenly as he started, Sherlock came to a stop and whined. He looked up at the row of lockers, yipped once, and promptly sat down. Figuring it was the proper thing to do, Watson did the same.

I looked at the lockers. Sherlock had stopped at #151. I tried to see if he wanted to explore the rest of the hallway, but the little corgi refused to be budged. That was all the affirmation Vance needed to pick up his cell and place a call.

Fifteen minutes later the janitor was there. Vance wordlessly pointed at the locker. The janitor grunted once, pulled out a familiar ring of keys, selected one at random, and unlocked the locker. He stepped out of the way and waited while Vance carefully inspected the contents.

Books, wadded up papers, pencils, two rulers, a spiral notebook that was almost ripped in half, and a moldy apple met our gaze. Vance carefully moved all the items to the floor and gingerly felt around the insides of the locker. He looked back at me and shrugged.

Nothing.

"Come on, Sherlock," I told the dog, patting his head. "There's nothing there. It's a false alarm. Let's look somewhere else, okay?"

Once more the corgi refused to budge. Sherlock turned to look at Vance and cocked his head. Vance met the corgi's gaze, grumbled once, and moved back to the locker to search again. The janitor stepped forward.

"Here. Use this."

It was a flashlight. Vance mumbled his thanks, clicked it on, and stuck his head in the small locker. It wasn't until he twisted around, looking straight up, that he grunted with surprise. He held the flashlight out, as though he was a surgeon looking to dispose of a scalpel he had been using. Once the janitor reclaimed his flashlight Vance reached an arm up into the top of the locker, yanked once, and came away with a false panel.

"Did you find it?" Tori hopefully asked. "Is the pendant in there?"

Vance pulled himself out of the locker, turned around, and held up a small sealed baggie of a dried green substance.

"No, but I did find some weed. That had to have

been what Sherlock smelled."

Jillian smiled warmly at the little corgi and ruffled the fur behind his ears.

"Good doggie. You found some drugs! Aren't you a smart, handsome boy?"

Sherlock regarded her as though she had asked him if he wanted a bath.

"Is that all that's in there?" I asked. I noticed Sherlock still hadn't moved.

Zack reached up into the tiny hidden compartment and felt around some more. After a few moments he pulled his hand out and handed the false panel to the janitor. He shrugged.

"That's all I could find."

"What about all that stuff on the ground?" I asked, pointing at the crap from the locker that was now spread out on the floor.

"Don't worry 'bout it," the janitor said. "I'll take care of it. I have to report this to the principal anyway. No drugs 'lowed on campus."

"I think you need to suggest that all lockers should be methodically searched," Vance told the janitor.

The janitor nodded. "I'll tell 'im tomorrow mornin'. He ain't gonna be too pleased about this."

As we were walking away, I still couldn't help but notice that Sherlock still refused to move. I could only assume that there was more marijuana hidden in some of the other lockers. But in close proximity to #151? I couldn't help but feel that we were missing something.

Turns out, I really should pay more attention to Sherlock and follow my instincts.

FIVE

The following Monday, I was in my kitchen, flipping angrily through the only cookbook I could find in the house. Consequently, it was a Betty Crocker cookbook that had been published in the mid-1950s. I know, I checked. I had seriously mucked up the first attempt at a date since my wife's death. I was hoping by offering to cook dinner I could mend a fence or two. Therefore I was desperately searching for a recipe that:

    a) Sounded good.

    b) Would taste just as good as it sounded.

    c) Had four ingredients or less.

Do you have any idea how complex those recipes are when you are not a cook? 'Gently fold in' this, or 'season to taste' that. When you don't know what you're doing in the kitchen, the only thing you want to see is a very explicit list of instructions.

Now, in case you're wondering about option 'c' up there, let me explain. I already told you that the kitchen is not my favorite room. My idea of a homemade meal was cooking one of those yet-to-be-baked pizzas that you finished yourself at home. However, Samantha—knowing that cooking was so far out of my comfort zone that it was considered to be the next county—encouraged me to try. Turns out that if the recipe called for four ingredients or less, then I could typically muddle my way through it. I should also mention that I consider spices as ingredients.

So, what did I end up settling on? 'Hungry Man Casserole', a dish my mother used to make for me all the time when I was a kid. The recipe actually called for five (gasp!) ingredients, fulfilling both options 'a' and 'b' at the same time. It had ground beef, pork and beans, cheese, and biscuits, which should satisfy option 'c'. If I managed to get through this without burning anything—or poisoning Jillian—then I'll definitely spring for a newer cookbook. I'll even let her pick it out.

I looked at the list of supplies I'd need if I had any hopes of pulling this off. Ground beef, pork and beans, barbecue sauce, grated cheddar cheese, and biscuits. Those were ingredients I could get on board with, even though barbecue sauce technically put this recipe over the four-ingredient limit. I didn't bother looking in the pantry or the fridge. I knew I had some barbecue sauce, but that was it. So it was off to Gary's Grocery.

I gingerly picked up my keys and eyed the sleeping dogs. Should I wake them up so I could take them with me? I decided against it. The grocery store was only about ten minutes away. I wouldn't be gone that long. I bet I could slip back in the house before either of them noticed I was gone.

A quick peek over the couch confirmed that neither corgi had moved a muscle. Sherlock had all four paws in the air and Watson was doing what I called the 'flying-squirrel' impersonation: both front legs were tucked close to her sides and her two short back legs were sticking out directly behind her. Both of the corgis were out cold. In fact, Sherlock was snoring.

I tip-toed out of the house, started up my Jeep, and hurried to the store. With my mind still squarely stuck in a kitchen from the '50s, I zipped through the store as though I was on a timed scavenger hunt. One can of pork and beans, check. Ground beef, check. Bag of shredded cheese, done. Tube of biscuits? Wow, there were a lot to choose from. However, I picked one that looked generic enough and tossed it in my cart.

Drinks. What about drinks? I knew Jillian wouldn't expect me to buy wine. She may enjoy a glass of white wine when in the company of other wine drinkers but for this date, she wasn't going to have to worry about that. I may need to acquire a taste for the stuff, but not today. I selected a bottle of sparkling grape juice and hurried off in search of other supplies I knew I needed.

Milk Bones. Bread. Rawhide chews. Peanut butter. I quickly filled the cart as I remembered various other things that I needed. A brief announcement over the intercom informed me of a sale happening in the store's small bakery, donuts. A baker's dozen for only five bucks. My cart automatically veered toward the far corner of the store. However, a commotion outside brought me to a screeching halt.

People were shouting. I even heard a scream or two. I then heard Gary himself get on the overhead paging system to announce that there was no need to be alarmed. The store owner almost seemed glad to be able to announce that the police had been notified.

Have you ever heard an announcement like that and NOT been alarmed? I abandoned my cart and hurried to the outside windows. There were a few people rushing around, pointing frantically at something I couldn't see. I could also see that quite a few of the store's patrons had also abandoned their purchases and had made a beeline straight for their cars.

Just then a woman, pulling a wailing little girl behind her, hurried into the store. She was trying to comfort the girl and carry on a conversation with someone on her cell phone at the same time.

"No, honey, it's alright. Mommy is fine. We're safe in here. Peter? I'm not going back outside until you get here … No, I'm not being silly. I saw it this time … No, I'm not making that up. I'm not taking Emily anywhere near that mummy."

My head jerked up. The mummy? It was here?

"Where was it?" I interrupted, as I saw the woman take a breath. "Did you get a good look at it?"

The little girl tugged on her mother's hand.

"Mommy, I hafta go to the baffroom!"

"Emily just a minute. Peter, I'm serious! Hang on a moment. Excuse me? What did you ask me?"

I blinked with surprise. The last question had been directed at me.

"Sorry to interrupt, but did you say you saw the mummy?"

"I most certainly did," the woman confirmed. "It was just outside, across the street. It saw me watching it and it ran down Main, toward 8th Street."

"It ran away from you?" I repeated, incredulous.

My faith in the bandaged desperado from the 18th Dynasty just took a major hit. Anger flared. Anger and embarrassment. Vance had been right. Mummies do not become reanimated, no matter how much you might like to think otherwise. Someone was pranking us and that someone needed to be caught.

"Which way did it go?" I anxiously asked.

The woman, more interested in arguing with her significant other than answering my question, ignored me. I looked down at the little girl who had finally stopped crying and was now sniffling miserably next to her mother's side.

"Do you know which way the mummy went?" I

gently asked the girl.

Emily nodded, wiped her nose with the back of her hand, and pointed north, toward 8th Street.

I smiled at the girl. "Thank you!"

I looked north, toward all the commotion. People were running, terrified, in every direction but north. I couldn't blame them. Every fiber in my being wanted to turn tail and run the other way, too.

Is that what you really want to do?

I paused. It was Samantha's voice. It had sounded so real that I momentarily thought she might have been at my side.

This fear is irrational, a new voice said. You're better than this. You know full well there is no way a mummy is responsible.

Great. The voice had switched to Vance's. Why was I imagining I was hearing voices?

Because you think a mummy came back to life, pal. Stop farting around here and get going. You have a chance to unmask this perp once and for all!

Think about the corgis, my inner voice advised, switching back to Sam's voice. What would you do if something threatened them?

That was an odd thing for my subconscious to dream up. Samantha had died before I had either of the dogs. She had never known them. I could only assume my imagination was trying to stimulate the senses in an attempt to get me to do something.

Well, it was working.

I had to know. I had to know once and for all if my fears were founded or if I was being pranked, which everyone seemed to think I was. I had a chance to get some answers and since I knew I was going to report this to Vance, I had to be able to tell him that I didn't chicken out and run the other way. So I did the only sensible thing I could think of.

I sprinted toward 8th Street, trying desperately to think of what lay in that direction. If I remembered the layout of the town correctly then this street was going to dead-end just past D Street into a heavily wooded lot. I knew the only thing out there was a large manor that had been converted into a hotel. Carriage House Inn & Suites, if memory served. And on the other side of that wooded lot?

The high school.

I ran harder. I briefly thought about pulling out my cell and calling Vance but thought better of it. I doubt I'd be able to wheeze out anything he'd be able to understand.

Zack + jogging = miserable Zack in need of a defib kit.

I made it to D Street. I glanced over and saw the elegant white mansion that had been renovated into a hotel. I was about to head in that direction when a loud cry of pain caught my attention. Thankfully it hadn't come from me. It had originated directly ahead of me. Somewhere within the woods.

I was now convinced I was pursuing the practical joker, and quite possibly, the idiot responsible for the theft of the necklace. Pendant. Whatever it was, I had a chance to apprehend the individual that I was certain either had a hand in the theft or else could point us in the right direction.

I ran into the trees, pausing only long enough to listen for signs of anything else that might be in there with me. Just up ahead, and slightly to my left, I heard a faint cough. As carefully and as quietly as I could, I crept toward the sound. If I could only rein in my own wheezes long enough, I should be able to tell which direction I need to go.

A twig snapped loudly nearby. I heard a muffled groan and a figure appeared nearly twenty feet away. Scraps of torn linen flapped in the breeze as the swaying form raised both arms up in proper "undead" fashion and shuffled toward me.

I gasped with alarm. It was the mummy, alright, and the thing was coming right for me! I was right all along! I had to prove it, but how?

A light bulb flashed over my head. I had my cell, which meant I had a camera. At the rate the mummy was moving I had about ten seconds to snap a picture and clear out.

With shaky hands I was able to pull my cell from my pocket, tap the camera app, and line up a shot. I tapped the screen and watched the camera's built-in video camera start recording the scene. Right about then, the mummy froze, hastily turned around, and retreated. In fact, it sprinted away from me, as though I had just lit one of the trailing pieces of linen on fire.

Vance was right. Jillian was right. So were the voices in my head. There was no mummy. It had been a prank after all, and based on the direction in which the impostor had fled, I'd say I had been duped by a high school student. The 'mummy' had bolted straight toward the school.

I already had my phone out so I hurriedly called Vance.

"Zack, what's going—"

"Vance!" I interrupted, trying hard not to wheeze into the phone, "Get to the high school!"

"I'm kinda busy here, buddy. There's been another sighting of this mummy, and I have to —"

"I know! I..." I took a few seconds to take a deep breath. "I chased him to the high school!"

"You what?!"

"I'll tell you all about it in person!" I wheezed a few more times before I could speak again. I just couldn't seem to catch my breath. "I'm in the woods by ... by ... that white hotel. He ran from me, straight... straight toward the high school. You gotta hurry, pal!"

"I'm on my way! I was just leaving the station. Be there in just a few! Do you see him now?"

I crashed through the woods, running as fast as I could.

"N ... no. Lost him ... he can't ... he can't be too much farther ahead!" I puffed.

I heard a siren wail in the distance and grow

progressively louder.

"Don't kill yourself trying to follow him. It sounds like you're about to have a heart attack."

"B... b... bite me."

"That's it. I'm calling for a paramedic."

"Kiss..." I wheezed, "kiss my a—."

I emerged from within the trees and stared at the huge parking lot in front of me. The high school had enough room to handle several hundred cars and since it was just before noon, all the students were in session. That meant several hundred cars were between me and the school. I groaned. There were plenty of places to hide.

Two cop cars came roaring around the corner with their lights flashing and sirens blaring. The police cars skidded to a stop and parked in a 'V' formation, effectively blocking the school's one and only exit. Vance came barreling out of the first car, caught sight of me, and rushed over.

"Zack! Are you okay?"

I clutched a painful stitch in my side.

"Y-yeah. I'm good."

"Where is he?" Vance anxiously asked as he looked at the vast parking lot full of all kinds of cars and trucks.

"All I can tell you is that he didn't make it to the school," I told him.

"How can you be so sure?" the other officer asked.

"Look how far it is from the edge of the woods there to the school entrance. There's no way he could cover that distance before I came out. He's gotta be hiding behind a car."

"Or his own car is parked in there somewhere," Vance suggested, eyeing the dozens and dozens of vehicles. "If he was dressed as the mummy then chances are, he's changing clothes as we speak."

I looked at Vance and put a friendly hand on his shoulder.

"I want to apologize. You were right. You knew all along that this was just some kid pranking us. You must think I'm the world's biggest moron."

Just then a loud bell started ringing in the distance. Almost immediately the school's front doors banged open and streams of students began pouring out. It was just our luck that we arrived just as the students were released for lunch.

Within moments students were everywhere. There was no way we were going to be able to find the mummy impersonator in the midst of at least a hundred students milling about. All he had to do was ditch the mummy getup—if he hadn't already —and disappear within the multitudes. Several students had even started their cars and were trying to leave the parking lot. Horns began blaring.

"What do we do?" the other officer asked, giving Vance a helpless look.

"Dammit," Vance grumbled. "That guy could be anywhere now."

"We should search the cars," the cop suggested. "If it was one of the students, then we should find his costume somewhere in one of these cars."

144

The line of cars was growing. More horns sounded angrily. Vance turned to me.

"Did you see the guy in the parking lot anywhere?"

I sadly shook my head. "No. Wish I did. From the way he was running, and the direction he was headed, he had to be going this way. However, I don't have any proof."

"We have to let them through." Vance groaned, turning to look at the angry faces of the students. "Come on, Dyson. Move your car."

Once the flow of traffic had been restored, Vance met my eyes and nodded toward the woods. The other cop had already left a few minutes earlier, as had nearly a third of the vehicles that had been parked earlier.

"I let the guy slip through my fingers," I groaned. "I could've had him, Vance. I can't believe we were thiiiis close to catching our friend the mummy."

"We nearly caught a kid that was dressed up as a mummy," Vance corrected.

"What difference does it make?" I asked. "Either way you look at it, the guy responsible for this whole mess is gone."

"Not necessarily," Vance contradicted. "I think what we have here is just a couple of stupid high schoolers trying to have some fun. I think the last thing he expected was to have you come tearing off after him."

"So what?" I argued. "It means you're right.

There's no mummy. I was a fool to think other-wise."

"Welllll….."

I turned to give Vance a disbelieving look.

"What? What is that supposed to mean?"

Vance shrugged and studied the ground. I coughed a few times but he wouldn't look up. Had something happened to change the detect-ive's mind? I was missing something. I tapped on Vance's shoulder and kept tapping until he finally looked up and swatted my hand away.

"What's happened?" I reiterated. "What aren't you telling me?"

"I think you're right, bud," Vance all but whis-pered. "I think you've been right all along."

"About what?" I asked, confused. "It's just a guess but I'm pretty sure the guy we're looking for is a student."

"The guy we're looking for is over 3,000 years old," Vance corrected, still refusing to meet my eyes.

"Wanna run that by me again?" I asked, certain I had heard that wrong.

"The mummy did this."

"I was running after a kid, who freaked out once he saw that I wasn't spooked. There's no mummy involved at all."

"Forget about the kid," Vance snapped. He quickly looked around to make sure no one but me could hear him. "Look, Zack, there's some-thing I haven't told you yet."

"I'm listening. What's up?"

"They've ID'd the body," Vance told me.

"The mummified dude?" I swallowed nervously. "Alright, who is it?"

"They took DNA samples from the body," Vance whispered. "While the tests aren't quite complete, they did find a likely match, Zack."

"Who?" I asked.

"It was a match to Fadil. Mr. Ammar Fadil."

I nodded. "Ammar. That's Dr. Tarik's assistant. I'm really sorry to hear that. Why haven't they completed the DNA tests yet?" I asked. "The lab can't be that busy, can they?"

"A proper DNA analysis can take several weeks, pal. I had the lab put a rush on this and am glad they managed to give us something."

"If you say so," I said, unconvinced.

Exasperated, Vance pulled me to his car. He pointed at the passenger seat as he slid behind the wheel. Confused, I slid into the seat.

"What's the big deal?" I asked. "Look, I'm sorry it was that guy's assistant, but at least they can't put any of this on Tori, right?"

"You're still not getting it," Vance crossly said as he pulled away from the school. "That body is —or was—Ammar Fadil, Dr. Tarik's assistant. With me so far?"

Growing annoyed, I nodded.

"Okay. Think back a couple of days ago to the night of the robbery. Do you remember what Dr. Tarik said about mummies? And how long it takes for a body to become dried out like that?"

"Desiccated," I quietly murmured to myself. My eyes widened. I was starting to see where my friend was going with this.

"Zack, he said it takes a minimum of thirty-five days for a human body to turn into kindling. We both saw Ammar a couple of days ago. Dr. Tarik says he last saw his assistant the day before yesterday. There is no way for a human body to become that thoroughly desiccated, unless..."

Vance trailed off and I swallowed nervously.

"You're not thinking what I think you're thinking, are you?" I asked.

Vance angrily shook his head. "Even if I think I know what you think I think you're thinking, then you still can't deny the obvious."

I held my hands up in a timeout gesture.

"Wait. You threw in way too many 'thinks' in the same sentence."

"You can't overlook the obvious," Vance explained. "There's too much evidence to suggest otherwise. There's simply no way a human body can look like that in only a few days. I think ... well, I mean, the mummy must have..."

"How did I become the devil's advocate?" I demanded, confused and bemused at the same time. "I'm the one who thought the mummy was real, only to learn it was a fake. Now you're telling me that you think the mummy is real and is responsible for killing Ammar? How?"

Vance drummed his hands on the wheel. He

mumbled something, but it was too low for me to make out.

"What was that?" I asked.

"Well, it's possible."

"How?" I demanded. "How would you know?"

Vance shrugged. "I saw it in a movie."

"Forget about the movies," I told my friend. "You're a detective. From what I can see, you're a pretty good one. So, start detecting. What else could it be? How could that body have become mummified in only two or three days?"

"It couldn't," Vance decided, with a sigh.

"So what other scenarios could explain it?" I asked.

"None I can think of," Vance sadly admitted.

"You told me over and over that there wasn't any mummy involved," I reminded Vance, waggling a finger at him. "I'm telling you now that there is some type of rational explanation for this. We just have to find it."

"We?" Vance asked, turning to look at me.

I nodded. "Yes. We. You, me, and Sherlock. Watson, too, if she feels like it."

"A part of me feels like we're going after a real mummy," Vance quietly admitted.

"I double-dog dare you to say that to Tori," I challenged.

"Are you kidding me? She has enough on her mind to worry about."

"Then what are you planning on doing?" I asked. "You must have something in mind."

Vance nodded. "I do. What are your plans for tonight?"

I shrugged. "Nothing I can think of. I was … oh! Jillian! I was in the process of buying some stuff to make for dinner tonight!"

"You cook?" Vance skeptically asked.

"Not well," I admitted. "Give me a cookbook to follow and I can usually muddle my way through. Usually, that is."

"Think Jillian would be up for a nice walk?"

I had started shaking my head the moment Vance had asked if I had anything planned for the night.

"Dude, no. I'm not doing this to her two dates in a row. I'm trying to make amends for the last one. I can't even begin to imagine what it would take to pull myself out of the doghouse for ruining her night. Again. Wait, what? You want to go for a walk?"

"I need to redeem myself," Vance admitted. "I might have let it slip that the two of us almost got lost in the maze. Tori thinks it'd be therapeutic if I tackle it again."

"You want to take on that corn maze again? Seriously? Why on earth would you want me in there? I'm even more useless than you'd be."

Several hours later I would be fervently wondering if The Apple Blossom stocked enough flowers to cover the debacle the evening would become. Thankfully, though, it wouldn't be me in the doghouse. This time.

SIX

I will admit that you had me worried," Jillian told me that evening. "Any recipe that includes pork and beans as well as barbecue sauce usually raises my red flags. I want to say that I was wrong. Your casserole was really good, Zachary."

"No offense was taken," I assured her. "Cooking is not my forte. However, give me a simple recipe to follow and I can usually hold my own. Besides, I grew up eating this type of food."

"And you remembered the recipe off the top of your head?" Jillian asked, impressed. "Good for you!"

I finished putting the dishes in the dishwasher, dried my hands, and reached behind the toaster to slide out the old cookbook I had found.

"Not exactly. I had some help."

Jillian picked up the book, blew off a layer of dust, and hesitantly opened it.

"Oh, Zachary. Is this the only cookbook you have? I am so sorry. Come by my store. The first new cookbook you pick out is on me."

"Don't laugh. I think my mom had this very

same cookbook. Maybe a few years newer, but I know I remember seeing something like that back when I was growing up."

"Do you miss her?" Jillian asked. "Didn't you say that all of your family still lives in the Phoenix area?"

I nodded. "Yes. My parents are in Scottsdale, my sister is in Goodyear, and I have a brother in Gilbert."

"Do they have kids?" Jillian asked.

"My sister has one son and my brother has two boys and one girl. What about you? You said you've lived in PV all your life. Does that mean your parents live here, too? Any siblings?"

"I have an older brother, Joshua," Jillian told me. "He's a marine, in the military. As for my parents, you're right. They live here, too, only not at the moment."

"Are they snowbirds?" I asked. "Do they have a house somewhere else?"

"They bought themselves an RV and are, at present, somewhere in Idaho. They stopped at a little town called McCall. Apparently, there's some great fishing up there."

"That must be fun for them," I said, as I finished drying dishes. "Being able to see the country at their own leisure is something I think most of us would like to do at some point. When do you expect them back?"

Jillian shrugged. "Spring of next year, maybe summer. I told them there's no rush.'

"Well good for them."

"You're stalling," Jillian accused, giving me one of her stunning smiles.

"No, I'm not."

"Then just ask me."

"Ask you? Ask you what?"

"To go with you to the maze tonight. I know the Samuelsons are going to be there."

"What is it with women?" I groaned aloud. "Do they always tell each other everything?"

"Tori is one of my best friends. That means I got to listen to how Vance nearly got the two of you lost in the maze." Jillian laughed and shook her head, sending her brown tresses tumbling about. "I don't understand how you two could've gotten so mixed up. Didn't Vance use the cheat sheet he was given?"

I shrugged. "Well, yeah, but it didn't matter. I can't believe he wants to go again."

"Are you up for this?" Jillian asked mischievously.

"Wait, are you saying you want to do this? Take on the maze, that is."

"Sure! I go every year. I'd love to go with you. You can help me beat my personal best time of about fifty minutes."

I stood up and reached for my wallet and cell.

"You're on. Let's see. It's 5:30 p.m. now. It'll take us at least fifteen minutes to get to Fanny's Farms. Let's just round that up to 6 p.m. That'll give us about an hour before it gets dark. Do you think we can solve it before it gets too dark to see?"

I extended a hand and pulled Jillian to her feet. She beamed a smile up at me.

"Let's go find out, shall we? I just need to get my purse. Have you seen it?"

I pointed back at the couch. The only part of the purse that was visible was part of the shoulder strap. The rest was concealed underneath one of two very upset looking corgis. Sherlock was watching us, with both ears straight up. Somehow the little booger knew we were planning on leaving.

"I need you two to watch the house for a couple of hours, okay?" I instructed the two dogs. "You're gonna be on your own. Try not to get into…"

I trailed off as I watched Sherlock glance once at Watson, and then together they jumped down from the couch. Both corgis trotted over to the door, turned back around to face us, and plunked both of their butts down. There was no way to get outside the house without dealing with their royal highnesses.

"Looks like someone wants to go," Jillian observed.

"They aren't invited," I told Jillian, turning to frown at the dogs. "They … aww, come on. That's not fair."

I watched as two sets of furry ears slowly drooped. If possible, both corgis adopted even more mournful expressions and slid into down positions. Sherlock rested his head on his front paws and stared at me, unblinking. Watson gave a low, piteous whine.

"Fine. You win. You two can come."

In less time that it takes to blink an eye, both corgis were back on their feet, barking excitedly, and running laps around us. Sherlock finally hesitated long enough to nose one of the leashes that I keep hanging by the door. Properly secured, we all stepped outside and headed toward my Jeep.

Both Sherlock and Watson fidgeted the entire time we were driving, running from one side of the back seat to the other, yipping excitedly. I've driven with the dogs a number of times now. I've never seen them this excited before. You'd think I was taking them for an outing to a dog park. I turned to Jillian, but was surprised to see her watching me.

"What?"

"I was just thinking about how much you remind me of Michael."

I reminded her of her dead husband? I didn't know if that was meant to be taken as bad or good. Without realizing it, I frowned. Before I could say anything, Jillian placed her hand on mine, which was currently on the gear shift.

"Oh, no, I don't mean anything bad by that. I'm so sorry. What I should have said is that you and Michael share a lot of common traits. You're both kind, you both love animals, you're both tall. The list goes on and on. It's almost spooky sometimes."

"Good spooky or it-creeps-the-bejeezus-outta-me spooky?"

"Good spooky," Jillian giggled. "What about me? Do I remind you of your wife?"

I hesitated. What was the best way to answer? Truthfully or make something up? I opted for the truth.

"Er, no. Sorry."

"That's okay, Zachary. Seeing how painful it is for you to think about your wife, I'm glad I'm nothing like her."

We pulled up to Fanny's Farms. While not necessarily packed, there were a lot of cars in the makeshift parking lots. The eatery had a line ten people deep and the small gift shop was overrun with tourists. A local radio station was playing over strategically placed loudspeakers and, I'm sorry to say, I could hear an occasional whistle blast from a directionally-impaired maze runner. Might as well get this over with.

I bought two tickets for the maze. We had some time to kill before we were due to meet up with Tori and Vance so we headed to the back of the farm's gift shop where we could see that nearly a dozen tents had been set up. This farm, like the first I had seen, had vendors selling all manner of things. Not really sure what to expect, I jammed my hands in my pockets and followed Jillian into the first tent.

I grunted. This tent had rack after rack of hand

decorated Christmas ornaments. While pretty, they really didn't do anything for me. So I pasted an obligatory smile on my face and made appropriate oohs and aaahs whenever Jillian held an ornament up for my opinion.

The next tent had mini tombstones. I blinked and looked again. Yep. Anyone who considers him/herself to be a true Halloween enthusiast will most definitely need to consider getting your very own personalized gravestone to decorate your house. Judging by the look of surprise on Jillian's face, this must be the first time this particular vendor had set up shop in Pomme Valley.

The next stall definitely caught Jillian's attention. The lady inside this tent was selling hand-decorated eggs. Not just chicken eggs, mind you, but everything from ostrich eggs all the way down to what I was told was a hummingbird's egg. They had been hollowed, colored with some of the most ornate patterns I had ever seen, and some even had designs cut into the shell's surface. Confused, I gently picked up a chicken egg that had a significant part of its shell cut away and studied the miniature diorama that was visible inside. A teeny tiny polar bear was sitting on its rear next to what looked like a snow drift. It even looked like it was drinking a bottle of soda.

"That's cute," Jillian observed, coming up from behind me to try and look over my shoulder. It didn't work. She was too short and I was too tall.

"I never knew you could cut through an egg

shell like it was paper," I commented, looking around the display stands. "I mean, look at that one. It has bright, sharp colors and a really cool geometric design over every square inch. How is that even possible?"

"It's a 'pysanka'," an older woman's voice said.

Jillian and I looked up. A friendly looking elderly lady was standing directly on the other side of a large glass display case and was smiling at us. She looked down, saw the two dogs, and automatically pulled out a bag of doggie treats. Two fuzzy canine derrieres hit the ground even before the bag could be opened.

"How do you make something like that?" Jillian asked, pointing at an egg that was larger than a chicken's. A goose egg, maybe?

"I start with raw eggs," the shopkeeper said, dropping several treats on the ground. "I use a pysachok to draw designs onto the surface using beeswax."

"Does it take a long time?" I asked.

The woman nodded. "As long as you can imagine and even then, sometimes longer."

I decided to buy an egg and started reaching for the polar bear design I had noticed earlier when I saw that Jillian had also selected one. Unfortunately, hers was bigger. Not to be outdone, I waited for her purchase to be wrapped up before I selected an even larger egg—an emu as I learned later—and tried not to groan when I saw the price tag. It was $149! Oh, well. I'll chalk it up to helping support the local economy.

I ran our purchases over to my Jeep and returned in time to hear Jillian announce it was time to meet our friends at the maze's entrance. I held my arm out and waited for Jillian to slide hers into mine. With each of us holding a leash, we headed toward where I remembered the entrance to be. Jillian patted her shirt and winked at me. I knew she had tucked her borrowed whistle under her jacket. I, for one, surreptitiously slid a hand into my left back pocket. I felt the folded piece of paper and smiled. Good. My cheat sheet was still there.

Come on. You really didn't think I'd leave that behind, did you? That sheet is worth its weight in gold, provided I had someone better than me trying to follow it. I just hoped I didn't have to use it.

Vance and Tori were waiting for us at the maze's entrance. I smiled. There was a gorgeous German Shepherd sitting complacently by Tori's right side. He was staring straight at us. Well, straight at the corgis, if you want to get technical. Sherlock caught sight of Anubis and yipped a greeting. Anubis dropped down into a playful dog pose and barked back. Watson elected to remain by my side.

"I'm so glad you brought your dogs!" Tori exclaimed, squatting down to ruffle Sherlock's ears. Watson pushed by me to secure her own bit of attention. After scratching under Watson's chin for a few moments, Tori straightened, inclined her head at the entrance in the rows of corn, and held out her hand. I heard Vance groan as we all stepped inside.

"Feels like we were just here, doesn't it?" Vance quipped as we followed a teenage couple into the heart of the corn field.

Since Halloween was just around the corner, both of the teenagers were wearing costumes. The girl was dressed as Little Bo Peep while the guy was some type of zombie with a fake knife through his head. Have I mentioned that I'm not a fan of dressing up?

"I can't believe this is your idea," I muttered as I came up alongside Vance.

"What?" he asked.

"The fact that we're back in here," I answered.

"Oh. Yeah, it kinda is. I've never had such crappy luck when navigating my way through a maze. I can only assume that your lousy sense of direction was starting to rub off on me."

"So this is round two, is that it?" I asked, grinning at my friend.

Vance nodded. "Yep. Man versus maze, take two. This time we'll get it right. In case we don't, however, do you ... that is to say, did you by any chance happen to bring the, umm..."

"The cheat sheet?" I whispered. "You bet I did."

"Good man, Zack," Vance exclaimed, slapping my back.

For the next thirty minutes we all laughed, explored, and got hopelessly lost—again—but you know what? None of us cared. We were all having a great time. We even had that young teen couple from before start to follow us around 'cause I figure they knew we had a better chance of finding our way out than they did. Jillian later told me that she overheard the girl tell the boy that she thought the dogs were cute.

As I said, things were going well for thirty minutes. Thirty-one minutes passed and things took a turn for the worse. Let's see if I can remember what happened in the order they happened.

First off, Sherlock stopped, dropped his nose to the ground and sniffed. His ears snapped up and his hackles rose. He looked straight ahead at the endless rows of corn and growled. Within moments all three dogs were growling and I'm fairly certain only one had reason to.

Second, it got eerily quiet. I looked at Jillian with a questioning look. She shrugged. At least she had noticed the absence of noise, too.

And finally, the four of us noticed we were now alone. None of us could remember the last time our group had come across any other runners. We had even lost the teen couple who had been shadowing us for the past half an hour.

"Did we make a wrong turn somewhere?" Vance asked, looking pointedly at me. "Where has everyone gone?"

"I'm more interested in knowing what set Sherlock off," I added.

"It looks as though he's pulling on his leash," Jillian observed. "Let's see where he wants to go."

Sherlock promptly led us deeper into the maze. At least we were still following a path through the maze. It was one of my deepest fears that we'd move beyond the actual maze and would stumble blindly about in a huge field of corn.

We rounded a corner and saw three Styrofoam gravestones. Another bend had a series of 'cob-webs' stretching across several stalks of corn. By the time we rounded the third bend, we started seeing people again. We saw a family of Fran-kensteins. Yeah, literally. The entire family was dressed up as the same thing. Daddy Frankenstein, mommy Frankenstein, and two little girls. Both Frankensteins. Then we saw another family who looked like the Addams family, which I thought was cute. I briefly looked behind me as we passed just to see if either of them were Zora Lumen.

Right about then a group of teenagers walked by. Most of them were girls. Of the five girls, four were dressed like Josie and the Pussycats. The fifth was wearing a short plaid mini skirt with a white long sleeve blouse. The lone boy amongst the group of girls was dressed as an Egyptian pharaoh.

As the group of kids passed us by, Sherlock paused only long enough to woof a warning. Once the giggling girls had vanished from sight, the tri-colored corgi resumed his growls and led us far-ther away. Watson and Anubis had stopped their own growls but were following Sherlock closely, as if to assure the little corgi that they had his back should the situation call for it.

"I've never been able to understand why a young girl would want to dress like a slutty schoolgirl for Halloween," Jillian mused. "No one is scared of a schoolgirl."

I reluctantly raised a hand, "Not true. I wouldn't want to be in a room full of teeny boppers. Are you kidding me? That's the stuff of nightmares!"

Vance laughed, but he was cut off the moment Tori smacked his gut.

Five minutes later, we passed what I was certain was the place where we had found the dead body from a few nights ago. The dead mummified body, I reminded myself. I thought Sherlock would stop and at least check the area out. Nope. He glanced over as we passed the large clearing that had recently been cut into the corn but didn't even break stride. As we came upon the same junction point as we had before, with at least seven paths heading off in different directions, another group of kids appeared in a path coming from the north. All three were dressed as mummies.

There was no other way to describe what happened next but to simply say Sherlock went totally crazy. He began barking and there was nothing friendly about it. His hackles had risen, his teeth bared, and if I hadn't been holding onto the leash, I'm sure he would have torn off after the kids.

Just then, the unexpected happened. One boy took one look at us, cried out in alarm, and fled back up the path. The four of us shared a look. What had just happened?

The two remaining kids looked uncertainly amongst themselves before they turned tail and fled, too.

Sherlock was nearly frothing at the mouth. He was pulling so hard on his leash that he was almost choking himself. He wouldn't stop barking!

"Sherlock! Be quiet! What's gotten into you? You've seen all those other kids dressed up. Why would those three bother you?"

"They were dressed as mummies," Vance said as he frowned. "Were those the only mummies that we've seen so far?"

Jillian shook her head. "No. We saw one just as we went inside the maze."

"Remember the boy and girl that followed us around for a while?" Tori asked. "The boy was dressed as a mummy. Sherlock didn't have a problem with him."

My eyes widened.

"One of them has gotta be our mummy impostor! And I'm betting it was the boy who fled first! That's why Sherlock was growling. He must have picked up the same scent he smelled at the high school. What do you want to bet that kid knows where the pendant is?"

"Give me Anubis!" Vance demanded, thrusting his hand backwards. Tori tossed the dog's leash to him. "Anubis, find them! Go!"

Anubis took off like a shot. Vance let out a whoop and gave chase. Both Sherlock and Watson barked excitedly and pulled on their leashes. Clearly, they wanted to join the chase.

"Nuh uh," I told the corgis. "We'll follow at a more respectable distance. This is a matter for the police, not for us."

Sherlock whined and tried to get me to pick up the pace. Somewhere up ahead I heard Vance let out a shout. I looked back at Jillian. She was already pulling her whistle out.

"Good. Jillian, get some help. I don't trust this. Tori, take Watson. Sherlock and I are going to see if Vance needs any help."

I gave Sherlock some extra leash and we both took off. I let the corgi lead for a few minutes until we saw something lying discarded in the middle of the path. Scraps of linen. It was the kid's mummy costume. By some strange coincidence there was a mummy propped up like a scarecrow nearby.

Vance arrived a few minutes later. Unfortunately, he was empty handed. Somehow, that little puke had gotten away. Again!

"I take it you lost him?"

"Yeah, but I got something even better."

"What's that?" I asked.

"His looks. I saw him. I'll work with a police sketch artist and come up with a picture. He's a young little punk. I'll bet you a thousand bucks that our perp is a student at the high school."

"Look around us, pal," I told Vance. "We're in the middle of a stupid corn field. There's nowhere to run to. We should be able to find him."

"Are you kidding me?" Vance asked, incredulous. "The maze itself is 40-acres. Fanny's Farms must have over two hundred total acres. They could be hiding anywhere."

I promptly pointed down at the two dogs.

"I'll bet one of them can find him."

"They're not bloodhounds," Vance pointed out. "Besides, we don't have the perp's scent."

"Yes, we do," I corrected. "The costume! I'm pretty sure the kid dropped the costume back there."

"He did? How did I miss that? Zack, show me. Hurry!"

We rushed back to the wadded-up pile of white linen. I pulled my multi-tool from my belt, unfolded the pliers, and gently picked a piece of it up and held it out to Vance.

"Does this look like what the kid was wearing?"

Vance nodded. "Yes. That's it, alright. I wonder why he dropped it. No matter. This is perfect. If we can get ... is that blood?"

Vance took my pliers and held up a few strips of fabric. Sure enough, we could see several dark red smudges on the tattered scraps of cloth, as though someone had used the linen to wipe their bloody hands off. The detective held the strips down for the dogs. Anubis sniffed the costume, dropped his head down to sniff along the ground, and then looked pointedly in the direction the kid had fled.

I took my pliers back and held the strips down for Sherlock to sniff. Turns out my corgi wasn't interested in the costume at all. He was, however, anxiously pulling on his leash, wanting to go in the direction the perp had taken.

Anubis barked. It was all Vance could do to keep the big German Shepherd in place. After a few moments my detective friend squatted, as though he was going to release the dog, when I laid a hand on his shoulder.

"There was blood on the costume. One of them might be armed. Do you want to run the risk of hurting Anubis?"

"He most certainly does not," a woman's voice flatly declared.

We turned to see Tori and Jillian approach, with Watson trailing behind.

"Don't even think of turning him loose," Tori warned. "You're not going to put my dog in danger. If you want him to track somebody, then you go with him."

Vance nodded and looked down at Anubis. He ruffled the big dog's fur.

"You heard her, Anubis. Let's go find him!"

The German Shepherd took off like a shot. Vance was practically dragged behind him. I looked back at the girls and made a quick decision.

"Keep Watson safe. Sherlock, let's go!"

SEVEN

I hope you have a plan in place in case things get ugly," I shouted at Vance as we ran through the maze at breakneck speed.

"I do," Vance shouted back as he was half dragged through a wall of corn by Anubis. He had to wait until he wasn't pushing through eight-feet-tall corn stalks before he could continue. "If it gets ugly then I expect you and Sherlock to clear out of the way. Protect yourself, Zack. Promise me!"

"Don't you worry about me," I wheezed. "I'll be diving out of the way at the slightest sign of violence. Both of us will."

The path turned north. The kids we were following must have thought that making their own path through the maze was all it'd take to lose any pursuit. Anubis immediately led us down the narrow path. The German Shepherd barked a few times and broke out into another run. I couldn't stop the groan from coming out. Not only had I not been able to catch my breath, but from the way this was going, I wouldn't be any time soon.

Thankfully, my groan of dismay was lost to the sounds of us crashing through the corn stalks.

After running pell-mell through the maze for another minute or two, I realized where we were headed. If memory served, we were now angling toward that tiny road just outside the border of the maze. The road that's not supposed to exist.

"I think I know where we're going!" I called out. "Remember the road Sherlock found the other day just outside of the maze? I think those kids are headed that way!"

"Are you sure?" Vance asked. Anubis continued to bark and pull at his leash.

"Pretty sure." I managed to pull the map from my back pocket and snapped it open as I ran. "Look, the border of the maze is the outline of the continental US. I'm pretty sure that's what we're on now. We've got to be nearing the top here."

As if he had heard me, Anubis veered off the path and led Vance straight into the heart of the corn field. There were no paths, no openings or clearings. Nothing but acres and acres of swaying stalks of corn. Sherlock didn't hesitate. He immediately followed. A few moments later we found it. Two tire trails, stretching off to the east and west and a narrow path that would barely allow a compact car to pass. Vance pulled out his cell.

"Dispatch, this is Detective Vance Samuelson. I am in pursuit of a suspect just outside of the maze at Fanny's Farms ... Yes, that's the one. I want units covering every road leading away from this farm.

I … what? I don't know. There's gotta be several. Cover 'em all. The perp? Young. I'm guessing … I'm guessing he's a high schooler. Of course I'm out of breath. I'm running, you knucklehead. Get them in place. Out."

Vance thrust his cell back into his pocket and doubled his efforts. Now I feel I should point out that in order to become a police officer you had to go through training. You had to be able to chase the bad guy. Hell, I even knew that Vance liked to run for fun. As a matter of fact, he was always trying to get me to join him. However, unless there's some type of predator on my tail, there's no way you'll ever see me run for the sheer joy of it. Anyway, the point I'm trying to make is you have to be in great physical shape if you want to keep wearing a badge.

Why am I telling you all of this? Because Vance and Anubis were pulling ahead of me. By leaps and bounds. I may not be in perfect physical shape, but I could usually hold my own. Jeez, not against those two. I'm pretty sure Sherlock and I felt (and looked) like Laurel and Hardy next to those two.

An object came seemingly out of nowhere and smashed into my chest, knocking me backwards a full five feet. I landed on the ground—hard—and tried to blink the stars out of my eyes. A headache erupted and I tasted blood. My blood. What the hell happened?

Two arms appeared and pulled me to my feet. I swayed like a newborn giraffe as I tried to regain my balance. I felt a furry nose nuzzle my legs.

"Zack! Are you alright?"

The twinkling stars continued to obscure my vision. I blinked stupidly at Vance a few times before I asked what happened. Or at least I tried to.

"Muh ... wha..." I angrily cleared my throat. "Wha- what happened? What got me? Am I hit?"

"You ran into me, pal."

"That was you? Dang. I need to hit the gym. Why'd we stop?"

Vance pointed at Anubis. The big German Shepherd was standing as still as a statue. Sherlock sauntered over to lend a hand. Within moments both dogs were sniffing along the ground. Anubis suddenly looked off to the right while Sherlock kept his nose pointed straight ahead.

"They've split up," Vance explained, barely winded. "Anubis and I will take the right. You and Sherlock keep going straight."

"And what if we find something?" I asked, frowning. "What if the little punk is armed?"

"I seriously doubt it," Vance said. "But if he is, exercise extreme caution. Don't confront. Memorize his face, features, and anything else that stands out to you."

I nodded and took a couple of deep breaths. I was so tired, so out of breath, that I briefly wondered what Vance would think of me if I barfed right in front of him. I think it was becoming clear that I needed to start using my elliptical machine again. I clutched a painful stitch in my side and managed to wheeze out, "You ... you got it. Sherlock, let's go."

"Are you okay?" Vance asked, concerned.

"I'm fine. The first round is on whoever doesn't catch a bad guy first."

Vance grinned. "You're on!"

They took off like a shot. I gasped painfully a few times before urging Sherlock on. Let's face it. There's no way I was going to find one of those kids first. Heck, I'd be happy if I found anything. Sherlock's barking caught my attention. He was doing everything he could to wiggle out of his collar. I wrapped the leash around my hand a few times and scowled at the little corgi.

"Nuh-uh. No way. You're staying with me, amigo."

Sherlock yipped in exasperation. Little puke knows I can't keep up with him. Steeling myself for a lung bursting sprint through the corn, I gave Sherlock as much leash as I could without letting go of it.

"Okay, sport. You're up! Go! Do your thing!"

Sherlock looked at the fleeing forms of Vance and Anubis and whined. Apparently, the little fellow didn't want to become separated from his much larger companion. I gently tugged the leash to get his attention.

"Come on, Sherlock. We've got bad guys to find. You indicated someone went this way. Whataya say we go check it out?"

As if that was all the motivation he needed,

Sherlock barked excitedly and pulled me straight forward. I couldn't help but notice that he wasn't breaking out into a run. Could that mean he thought that the perp was somewhere nearby? Wouldn't that indicate the little punk was trying to hide?

I squatted down next to Sherlock and draped my arm around him.

"I think he's close, pal," I whispered to the corgi. Sherlock woofed softly in response. "He's hiding. We gotta find him. Think you can do it?"

Sherlock dropped his nose to the ground and began slowly inching forward. We made it about twenty feet when I noticed we had passed a cornstalk that was bent at an unnatural angle. A quick check confirmed it had been broken. Someone had recently passed it by! Excited, I grinned at Sherlock and urged him forward.

"We're getting close," I whispered to the dog. Sherlock's ears perked up. "He's here somewhere."

I don't know how Sherlock knows when I'm passing the leash from one hand to the next but the little booger timed it beautifully. Just as soon as I had unwrapped the leash from my right arm Sherlock surged forward, yanking the leash out of my grasp. His barks switched to the I'm-gonna-rip-your-throat-out variety and he took off. I managed to catch a glimpse of his fuzzy orange and black butt just as he disappeared into the rows of corn.

"Dammit, Sherlock! Get back here! Now!"

The sun had continued to set and I couldn't help but notice that it was now getting harder to see. I could really use a flashlight right about now. Wait. My phone! It had a simple app on it which would switch on the LED flash. One button press later my cell phone turned into a flashlight and, with the phone held high, I tried to follow Sherlock.

Just then I heard him bark. Almost immediately I heard a cry of pain. Not canine, mind you, but human. I anxiously surged forward. The last thing I needed was for that little punk kid to hurt Sherlock. What if he had a gun? What if he had already used it? Then again, if he had, I'd like to think I would've heard it.

After a few moments, following Sherlock's angry barks and the kid's increasingly frantic shouts, I found them. I was right. The kid looked to be around sixteen. He was short and skinny, had wild unkempt hair, and was sitting in the midst of several downed corn stalks. He had broken one off and was trying to keep Sherlock at bay. The corgi, on the other hand, looked determined to take a bite out of him. Sherlock was going absolutely crazy. He was barking his head off and bounding across the ground, as though the field we were in was now too hot to stand on. The kid took one look at me and relief washed over his features.

"Call off your dog, mister!"

"And who might you be?" I asked, ignoring the kid's request.

"Just call off your dog and I'll tell you," the kid pleaded.

I glanced over at Sherlock and saw that his teeth were bared and his hackles were up. I held up a hand to attract Sherlock's attention, intent on telling him to be quiet once he looked my way. However, much to my surprise, he fell silent as soon as he saw my hand in the air. He may have stopped barking, but it didn't look like he was planning on ceasing his growls any time soon. I reached down to grab Sherlock's leash, lifting it up to show the kid that I had it. I waited, expectantly, for the kid to start talking. Instead, however, the kid laughed and slowly rose to his feet. I thumbed my camera app and snapped a few pics.

"What'd you do that for?" the kid whined. "There was no need to take my picture!"

"Let's recap, shall we? You're hiding in the middle of a corn field. You're bleeding from your right hand and you have the audacity to insinuate you're just an innocent bystander here? Bull. Who are you? What's your name?"

The kid sniffed disdainfully and his nose lifted higher by a few inches.

"I don't have to answer your questions. I haven't done anything wrong. I'm leaving."

"You're not going anywhere," I assured the kid. "Don't want to talk to me? That's fine. We'll wait for my buddy to get here. You know, the other guy you're running from? He's a cop. A detective. I'm sure he'll be thrilled to meet you."

The kid gave a cry of alarm and pushed past me in an attempt to flee. Sherlock became a blur of motion. He darted in just as the kid was passing and bit him on the closest ankle he could reach. The kid howled with pain and went down, taking out a few more corn stalks as he did. He rolled into a sitting position while clutching his left ankle.

"Your dog bit me! I'm going to sue you, dude. I'm going to sue you for everything you're worth! Do you hear me? Wait, just wait a minute. Look, let's make a deal. Let me go right now and we'll each go our separate ways and I promise you I won't seek any legal action against you. Whataya say?"

"Do you think I just fell off the turnip truck?" I incredulously asked the teenager. "Why are you running? Could it be that you're one of the jerks who have been dressing up as the mummy to scare people? Am I right?"

"I don't have to talk to you," the kid snapped.

"Did you steal the mummy and the pendant, too?" I asked, growing angry. I was still wheezing like an old man, but I had forgotten all about how I couldn't catch my breath because of the simple fact that I had found one of the kids. Drinks are on you tonight, Vance. "Cough it up. Where did you hide them?"

"I didn't hide anything. You have no proof."

I turned to point at Sherlock.

"He's my proof. He hasn't stopped growling at you since he first met you. Sherlock would only do that if he recognized your scent."

The kid paled and a look of terror swept over his features. I knew right then that I had hit the nail on the head. This had to be the kid Sherlock had chased, back in the high school! For all I knew this was probably the same kid I chased through the woods but lost in the parking lot. You got away from me once, pal. Ain't *no way* I'm letting it happen again.

"So you're the one," I mused.

"I'm the one what?" the kid hesitantly asked.

"Sherlock chased you into the music room, didn't he?"

The kid's face paled even further. For a moment there I thought he was going to be sick.

"Ready to tell me who you are?" I asked again.

A firm resolve appeared on the teenager's face. He wasn't going to talk. In that case, maybe I ought to have a little fun with him?

"If you won't introduce yourself then maybe I will. My name is Zachary Anderson. That's Sherlock down there."

The kid's eyes widened. I grinned. Oh, this would work well. The kid had clearly heard my name before.

"You do realize that I was accused of murder a few months ago, right? They even found a body in my winery."

The kid gulped nervously but still refused to talk.

"Yessir, the body was found behind one of the

vats. Death by strychnine poisoning. I'm pretty sure the police will never know. It's hard to detect." I knew it wasn't, and that I was lying like crazy, but this kid didn't need to know that. "Do you have any idea what strychnine will do to a human body?"

Beads of sweat were trickling down the kid's forehead.

"You don't know? Oh, no problem. Let me explain it for you. Strychnine is an odorless, tasteless airborne virulent that causes some pretty painful symptoms. It can..."

At that moment Vance appeared, pushing a second teenage boy out in front of him. This boy, I noticed, had his hands cuffed behind his back. Anubis was less than a foot away, keeping pace with the sullen teenager as though an escape attempt could happen at any moment. A grin appeared on Vance's face the moment he spotted the kid on the ground. Nodding, he approached and held up a closed fist. I knocked his fist with my own and returned the grin.

"You rock, Zack," Vance told me as he pulled a second set of cuffs from a back pocket.

"You're off duty," I pointed out. "Do you usually carry around a set of handcuffs? Or, in this case, two sets?"

"Still have one more," Vance told me as he pushed his prisoner over to me. "Hold on to him for a second, would you? Little creep has tried to slip away three times now."

"So has he," I added as I pointed at my prisoner. "He wouldn't tell me his name."

"He doesn't need to," Vance told me as he pulled the kid to his feet. "I know full well who he is." The kid groaned and stared at the ground. "Zack, meet Jimmy Nelson."

"Nelson?" I repeated as I looked at the kid. "I know that name. Any relation to…"

"Yep," Vance cut in, before I could finish. "Young Jimmy here is Captain Nelson's grandson. And won't he be pleased as anything to know you're involved in all of this," Vance said, giving the kid a firm shake. "Captain Nelson can be quite intimidating. Wouldn't want to be you, kid."

"Oh, please don't tell him," the kid begged. "You have no idea how much trouble I'll get in if grandpa finds out."

Vance was unimpressed, "Can't do the time? Don't do the crime."

"Who's this?" I asked, pointing at the kid he had caught.

"He thinks I don't know who he is," Vance told me. "He's sorely mistaken."

"Then tell me what my name is," the second kid sneered. "Tell me what I'm being accused of. What's that? You can't? Oh, yes. I should have known. You can't prove any of it, so why don't you just get me to a phone. I'll be out in no time."

"Perhaps," Vance told the smug teenager. "Perhaps not. Either way, I'll see to it you're our guest for the next 96 hours. Except for you, Jimmy.

Something tells me your grandfather will want to have a word with you. And for the record, your name is Dean Rupert. Your dad owns..."

"You can't hold me any longer than twenty-four hours," Dean interrupted as he smirked. "It's the law."

"So you know something about law, do you?" Vance asked, not losing his own smile for even a second. "Then of course you know about murder suspects, right? If you're suspected of a serious crime, like a murder, then we can apply to hold you for 36 or 96 hours. Would you like to take a guess as to which direction we're going to go here?"

The smug expression vanished from Dean's face.

"What? Murder? You can't ... we didn't murder anyone!"

"We only stole some ugly old necklace!" Jimmy added. His face had turned as white as a sheet. "It was Dean's idea to take the mummy, too!"

"Shut your mouth, Jimmy! They don't have diddly squat on us. They can't prove anything."

"Whose locker is number 151?" I casually asked.

"Mine," Jimmy automatically answered. A moment later he was staring suspiciously at me. "Why?"

Well, that explained why Sherlock hadn't stopped growling at the skinny kid. It was his locker that he had singled out when we were back in the school. I now knew that he was the one that we had been chasing on the night of the robbery. No wonder Sherlock headed straight for his locker. He must have smelled him. Jimmy had already confessed to stealing the pendant. Was there something else in that locker that we had missed?

"Well, now we can add possession of a controlled substance to the mix," Vance added. "We found your stash of weed, kid."

"There wasn't any weed in my locker," Jimmy argued. "I don't smoke pot. Never have, never will."

"Yet we found several grams," Vance pointed out. "That's gonna look bad, Jimmy. If it wasn't yours, then it's high time to come clean. Whose was it? Was it Dean's?"

"I don't smoke pot either," Dean bitterly shot back.

"If it's not Jimmy's, and it isn't Dean's," I began, "then whose is it? Could it be the third kid's?"

"What third kid?" Jimmy asked, genuinely confused.

"You think there's someone else?" Dean added, throwing much of his sneer back into his voice.

"Were you, or were you not, with a third kid just now?" Vance asked as he pulled Jimmy to his feet.

"Rick?" Dean demanded. "Leave him alone. He's got no part in this. Besides, the kids in this town are too stupid to pull something like this off."

"Alright, let's go you two," Vance ordered, pushing Jimmy out in front. "You've caused enough problems for tonight. I gotta hand it to you both," my friend continued, laughing as he said so. "You sure had us going. You had the whole town thinking that a mummy had come back to life."

"We were just trying to have a little fun," Jimmy sulked. "We didn't hurt anyone."

"What about the guy who was killed?" I demanded. "What about that assistant fellow? Ammar? Remember him? How on earth did you manage to mummify a human in only a few days' time?"

Both teenagers stopped walking to stare at me.

"What are you talking about?" Jimmy asked, confused. "What body are you talking about? We didn't kill anyone."

"Explain the mummified body we found in the maze," Vance demanded. "That corpse sure didn't walk in here on his own."

"We didn't do anything to the mummy," Dean grumbled. "What's wrong with you, man? Why would you think it walked in here on its own?"

"Dean, we found a mummified body in this maze just the other night. You're telling me that you don't know anything about it?"

"A real mummified person?" Dean repeated, startled. "You're kidding."

"Dr. Tarik's assistant," I confirmed, eyeing both boys and wondering what their play was. "Ammar.

His body was mummified in true Egyptian fashion."

"We had nothing to do with that," Jimmy assured us. "I wouldn't even begin to know how to turn someone into a mummy."

"Likewise," Dean mumbled.

We headed back to the maze, intent on getting out of the claustrophobic cornfield as soon as possible, when we heard a siren approaching in the distance. Vance cursed silently, shook his head, and checked his watch. He pulled Jimmy to a stop and cocked his head at me.

"What?" I asked.

"That's gotta be the slowest response time I think I've ever seen. What, did they stop for donuts?"

I snorted in response.

"So where's this necklace, Jimmy?" Vance asked the sullen teenager. "Tell me where you've hidden it and I'll try to put in a good word for you with your grandfather."

Jimmy fidgeted from leg to leg. I got the impression that he wanted to tell us something, but was afraid of what Dean might say or do. Vance hooked a thumb in the direction of the approaching siren.

"The deal is off once they get here. Spill, kid. Where's the necklace."

Jimmy sighed and dropped his eyes to the ground.

"It's in my locker."

EIGHT

W hat on earth did you think you were doing?" Captain Nelson of the Pomme Valley Police Department demanded. He was one of eight people crowded into the small principal's office inside the high school. "Principal Reezen has every reason to expel you. To expel you both! And what is your mother going to say about this, Jimmy? Would you like to take a guess?"

"She'd say that you should arrest me," Jimmy sullenly answered.

I snorted softly. That was an understatement. The brat needed a serious reality check. From the looks of his livid grandfather, he was about to get it. I glanced around the room from my position in the doorway. Principal Reezen, two officers I didn't know, the two kids, Vance and myself were all watching a vein in Captain Nelson's forehead throb so much it was a wonder it didn't burst.

"You're absolutely right. Tell me why I shouldn't. Right now. Let's hear it."

Jimmy swallowed nervously, "Grandpa, you wouldn't really arrest me, would you?"

Captain Jason Nelson's hands kept clenching and unclenching. The look of outrage he had on his face when he looked at his grandson almost had me feeling sorry for the kid. Almost. I was just glad I wasn't on the receiving end of the interrogation this time around.

"You are going to tell me where that missing necklace is," Captain Nelson decided. "Right now. If you have any hopes for this little excursion to stay off your permanent record, then you'll confess, right now. And ... go."

"I already told you," Jimmy whined. "It's in my locker."

"Which number?" Principal Reezen asked, retrieving a familiar ring of keys from within his desk.

"151."

"Why did you steal that necklace?" Vance suddenly asked. "There were plenty of things that looked more expensive than that vulture thing. Why the pendant?"

Jimmy and Dean shared a quick look and both shrugged.

"You're going to do better than that," Captain Nelson ordered. "Detective Samuelson brings up a valid point. Whose idea was it to take that particular necklace?"

After a few moments of silence Principal Reezen cleared his throat.

"Let's up the ante, shall we? The first person to tell us the truth will face detention rather than expulsion. Who would like to go first?"

"Okay!" Dean cried. The teenager's smug demeanor was long gone. "You win. It was Jimmy's idea. This was all Jimmy's idea."

Jimmy hissed with irritation and refused to raise his eyes from the floor.

"He said that there was this necklace in the exhibit that was worth more than everything else combined," Dean frantically continued. "He said that we could sell that thing and make more money than we could ever make in a lifetime."

"They knew the pendant was authentic," I said, more to myself. Sherlock, stretched out on the floor next to me, glanced up at me, raising both ears as he did.

"What was that?" Captain Nelson asked, looking over at me.

"They knew the pendant was genuine," I repeated. "The question I'd be asking them is how they knew that."

Vance nodded. "Good point, Zack. Dr. Tarik said that he alone was privy to the true history behind that particular necklace."

Captain Nelson was silent as he considered. After a few moments he nodded and looked back at his grandson.

"Answer the question, James."

"I told you, grandpa. Don't call me that. I prefer Jimmy."

"Better get used to James, kid," Vance quipped. "That's the name that's gonna appear on your arrest record."

"Alright!" Jimmy exclaimed, jumping up from his seat. "It was me, okay? I was behind the whole thing! Is that what you wanted to hear?"

"You're also the one who stole the Egyptian Exhibitions' mummy?" Captain Nelson began. He was trembling with rage. "Do you have any idea how badly this reflects on PV? Why would you do this, Jimmy? Don't you have a single brain cell in your skull?"

Jimmy scuffed the toe of his foot on the linoleum-covered floor.

"What did you do with the mummy?" Principal Reezen asked. "Where have you two hidden it?"

"We didn't do anything to it," Jimmy insisted. "It's still safe. At least it was the last time I saw it."

"The last time you saw it?" Vance repeated. "Where is it, kid? This town is full of freaked out people. We need to make a show of retrieving the mummy and showing everyone that there's nothing animated about it."

"Good point," Captain Nelson conceded. "Jimmy, where is it?"

Jimmy sighed. "It's in the maze."

"At Fanny's Farms?" Vance asked, amazed.

"Yeah. I didn't want that creepy thing at my place, and Dean didn't want anything to do with it, so it was up to me to hide it. So I figured I'd stash it at the one place where no one would be surprised to find it."

"How could someone not be surprised if they came face-to-face with an actual mummy in the maze?" Principal Reezen asked, confused, as he turned to Vance. "Do you know?"

Vance shrugged. He didn't know. However, I did.

"The maze is decorated for Halloween," I reminded everyone. "There are already gravestones, giant spiders, fake caskets, and all manner of things around every corner in the maze. It wouldn't be surprising at all to see a mummy in there. In fact..." I trailed off as I remembered seeing a mummy propped up like a scarecrow during the chase through the maze. I looked around the room to see everyone staring at me. "I think I know where it is. When Sherlock and I were chasing after Jimmy we came across a mummy propped up like a scarecrow. It was near the scene of where we found that mummified person. Do you remember, Vance?"

Vance's head fell and he groaned.

"You found the mummified body?" Captain Nelson asked, his voice dropping dangerously low. He took a few moments to glare at Vance before turning back to me. "You and your dog? Interesting. I don't recall you mentioning that in your report, do you, Detective Samuelson?"

Vance shot me a dark look. "Uh, no sir."

Captain Nelson gave me a speculative look before dropping his eyes down to Sherlock. He smiled at the little corgi and shook his head. He walked over to Sherlock to give him a congratulatory pat on his head.

"That's a good boy."

Sherlock looked up at the captain and panted contentedly. The police captain looked back at me and nodded.

"You're certain you've seen the mummy?"

"I'm no expert," I told the captain, "but that one looked eerily authentic. Sherlock hesitated long enough to give the thing a second look, if it helps."

"Roger that. Very well. Jones, take Stidwell and check it out. If it's the real thing, then bring it back here."

Both of the cops, who hadn't said a thing up until this point, nodded. They exited the small office together. Captain Nelson then pointed to the two sets of handcuffs that were on the principal's desk.

"If either of you would like to avoid adding these to your permanent collection of jewelry, then you're going to tell me about the unfortunate Mr. Fadil. Now, if you..."

"Who?" Dean interrupted.

"Mr. Ammar Fadil," Vance clarified. "Dr. Tarik's assistant. He's the one who was mummified. Is any of this ringing a bell?"

"Why would you think either of us had anything to do with that?" Dean demanded.

"We didn't kill that guy!" Jimmy added.

"Then how is it the location you chose to stash

the mummy was in the same area as where we found Mr. Fadil's remains?" Captain Nelson asked. "Jimmy, I can't help you unless you're willing to help yourself. You need to come clean. How are you and Dean involved? I personally would like to believe that you aren't responsible. However, you are going to have to convince me. If you want my help then you have to help me."

"But grandpa," Jimmy whined, "I don't know anything about any dead body! Other than the mummy we stole, that is."

"What about you?" Vance asked, looking over at Dean. "What's your take on all of this?"

"Look, man," Dean began, "we stole the pendant. We smashed the display case and made it look like the mummy did it. That much we're responsible for. But we didn't kill anyone, let alone turn someone into a mummy. I mean, how do you think we could do something like that? Do you think they have 'how to make a mummy' videos on the internet?"

Vance turned to me.

"Do they?" he whispered.

I shrugged. I didn't know. I hoped not. That was the last thing I needed to worry about at this point.

"I'm still waiting," Principal Reezen announced, drawing everyone's attention.

"Waiting on what?" Vance asked.

"On how young mister Nelson here knew that the pendant was genuine. How did he know to take that one item when there were others that looked more appealing than that ugly vulture necklace?"

"Jimmy, did you know about the pendant's true history?" Captain Nelson asked, softening his tone as he did.

Jimmy hung his head. "Yes."

"How?" Jimmy's grandfather demanded.

"From a teacher, okay?"

A teacher? Uh, oh. I glanced over at Vance. He had the same look on his face as I did. He quickly looked my way. I could see worry etched all over his face. This didn't bode well. Was Tori responsible?

"Which teacher?" the principal wanted to know.

"My history teacher," Jimmy answered.

"Mr. Thompson or Mrs. Samuelson?" the principal asked.

"Mrs. Samuelson."

"Bull," Vance exclaimed. "She said she didn't tell anyone."

Several heads turned to stare speculatively at Vance. I groaned. Dude, if only you had kept your big trap shut.

"What was that, detective?" Captain Nelson dangerously asked. "Are you withholding information about this case?"

Vance gave a resigned sigh and nodded. "I'm afraid I am. Tori admitted to me that she figured out the true nature of that vulture pendant the moment it was put on display."

"And she told a classroom full of kids how a priceless Egyptian artifact was going to be in our small town?" Principal Reezen sputtered. His face had turned an ugly shade of dark red. "Is she insane?"

"She said she didn't tell anyone," Vance reiterated. "I believed her."

"What did your teacher say about the pendant?" Captain Nelson asked, turning back to his grandson.

"Well, nothing, if you want to get technical," Jimmy admitted.

"Hah!" Vance all but shouted. "I knew it!"

"But I did catch her researching that pendant several times on the computer," Jimmy continued. "I was curious. I wanted to know why she was so fixated on it. I remembered enough of what that thing looked like to look it up, too."

"And so you learned it was worth a lot of money," Principal Reezen deduced. "How, exactly, did you think you were going to move something like that? It's not like you could put it up on eBay."

"And that's why the pendant is still here," I guessed, smiling. Once again, I had drawn everyone's eyes to my own. "That's why they still have it. Now that they've got it, they've got no clue what to do with it. Am I right?"

Jimmy looked away with disgust. Dean glanced at his partner in crime and slowly nodded. Captain Nelson slammed a hand down on the desk, causing everyone to jump. Jimmy included.

"Dammit, Jimmy! Why would you do this? Do you have any idea how much trouble you're in? Why did you do it?"

Jimmy scuffed a shoe along the ground. "I was bored?"

Captain Nelson scowled again, looked over at Principal Reezen, and tapped the ring of keys, which he was still holding.

"Would you kindly examine the contents of his locker and tell me if the missing pendant is there?"

"We don't need to," Vance announced. "We already searched it yesterday. There was nothing there. Nothing but a bag of weed, that is."

"You're using marijuana now?" Captain Nelson all but roared as he sprang to his feet. "Of all the idiotic lame-brained stupid things ..."

"It's not ours!" Jimmy insisted. "I don't use pot, grandpa. Neither of us do. Someone had to have planted it! I swear!"

"If not you, then who?" Principal Reezen snapped. "Possession of marijuana is grounds for an immediate expulsion. The only reason we're even having this conversation and I'm not signing your expulsion papers is that your grandfather and I are old friends. Mr. Nelson, Mr. Rupert, if ever there was a time to come clean, it'd be now. Start talking."

I glanced over at young Jimmy to see what his reaction to that ultimatum was. The kid was looking straight at his grandfather and darned if he didn't try laying on the water works. Dean, on the other hand, looked as though he was ready to puke.

"Grandpa, I swear to you that weed isn't ours!" Jimmy was insisting. "I have no idea how it got there."

"Alright, everyone," Captain Nelson stated, rising to his feet. "We're going to end this right now. Jimmy, lead the way. You're going to return the pendant. Right now."

Jimmy's head fell as he resignedly pushed to his feet. Without looking at his partner in crime, he led us out of the office and down the hall, stopping only when he had reached his locker. Without asking for permission, he spun the locker's dial a few times and then stepped back out of the way. Principal Reezen pushed his way to the front of the procession, opened the locker, and immediately began dumping the contents onto the floor. Once the locker was empty, the principal turned to look back at Vance.

"Where did you find the marijuana, detective?"

"Above your head. If you turn around and look up at the top of the locker, you'll see a tiny notch in one of the corners. That's where the false panel was resting. Press on the small tab right there and the panel would drop down."

The principal was quiet as he inspected the insides of the locker. I watched him reach up into the top of the locker and grunt a few times, presumably as he ran his finger over the notch and the tab Vance had described. I caught sight of the police captain giving his grandson yet another disapproving frown, but young Jimmy had dropped his gaze to the floor and kept them there. Principal Reezen felt the insides of the locker wall for a few minutes more before finally turning around.

"This locker has been modified to hold a false ceiling. How? Who made these modifications? Where did you get that false panel?"

"Made it," Dean mumbled.

"Where?" the principal angrily asked. "How?"

"In shop class."

"With Mr. Eriksen's approval?" the head of the high school sputtered.

"No," Dean muttered. "The teacher didn't know anything about it. We done it on our own time."

"We did it on our own time," Principal Reezen hastily corrected.

"Whatever," Dean grumbled in response.

"The pendant isn't there, kid," Vance said, snapping his fingers to get Jimmy's attention. "Care to explain that?"

Jimmy sighed and pointed at his locker, "You're looking in the wrong place."

"Did you, or did you not, tell us that the pendant was in your locker?" Captain Nelson snapped. I noticed the veins on his forehead were becoming more and more pronounced. If ever someone was about to lose it, it'd be the captain.

"Yeah."

"Then where is it?" Principal Reezen asked.

"I told you they'd never find it," Dean smirked as he looked back at Jimmy. "I told you it was the perfect place to hide it."

I suddenly smiled. That's how the little punks did it. There was a second hidden panel.

"Check the bottom," I said to the principal. "I'll bet you there's another hidden panel, this time on the bottom."

Surprised, Principal Reezen turned back to the locker and swept candy wrappers, strips of paper, wadded up gum, and a myriad of other objects onto the hall floor. He peered at the bottom of the locker and grunted. I watched him reach inside with both arms and a few moments later he turned back around, holding a rectangular piece of metal.

"There," Jimmy grumped. "You have it back now. Are you happy? Can we go?"

"You're trying my patience, boy," Principal Reezen all but growled. "Is this some type of joke? Are you stalling for time? Trust me when I say it isn't going to work."

"What are you talking about?" Jimmy asked, growing agitated. "I told you where we hid the pendant. You've got it back. Everything can go back to the way it was. Please?"

"There's nothing there, Mister Nelson!" the principal bellowed. "The space below this panel is empty!"

I watched the color drain from Jimmy's face.

He lunged forward, pushing past both his grandfather and the principal. He stuck his head inside his locker to see for himself that his future was looking exceedingly dim. Jimmy angrily confronted Dean.

"You took it? You sneaky two-timing son of a bitch! How dare you! You would have never known about that pendant if it wasn't for me!"

"What are you talking about?" Dean demanded. "I didn't touch the thing."

Jimmy gestured angrily at the locker, "It's gone, Dean! You and I are the only ones who knew where it was hidden! I sure didn't move it. That leaves you!"

Dean pushed by his friend to stare down at the empty locker. Jimmy was right. The pendant was gone!

"Dude! Someone stole our pendant!"

NINE

"Let me see if I have this straight," Captain Nelson was saying. "You boys steal the pendant. And the mummy. You make it look like the mummy has come back to life to cover your tracks. You two are surprised to learn that it's not nearly as easy as it looks to try and find a buyer for a stolen pendant, especially one that is worth tens of millions of dollars. Therefore you stash the thing here. In a school. Only now the problem is that someone has stolen it from you."

"Yes," Jimmy all but whispered.

"And they've managed to get into your locker without you knowing."

"Yes," Jimmy said again.

"When was the last time you saw the necklace?" Vance asked. "When was the last time that you knew for certain it was there?"

"Yesterday," Dean answered. "Jimmy and I checked on it yesterday, after school."

"Is that true, Mister Nelson?" Principal Reezen asked.

Jimmy nodded. "Yes. We both saw it."

Vance nodded. "That means that whoever stole it from them did it sometime between 3:30 p.m. and ... and ... when does the school open in the morning?"

"Doors are unlocked at 6:00 a.m."

"When are they locked for the night?" I asked.

"There was a varsity volleyball game here last night," Principal Reezen said. "It would have lasted until about 8. Doors would have been locked by 8:30 p.m."

"Could someone have been able to get into Jimmy's locker before the doors were locked?"

"Are you suggesting another student is responsible?" the principal asked.

"I'm asking if there are enough people wandering the halls during the game that someone would have noticed a locker being forced open," Vance said.

"There were no signs of forced entry," Principal Reezen reminded us. "Whoever accessed that locker did so by either knowing the locker's combination or having the master key."

"Or, they could have picked the lock," I added.

Captain Nelson looked over at the principal.

"Don, is that possible? How easy would it be to pick the locks?"

Principal Reezen shrugged. "They're school lockers, Jason. Each locker is secured with a standard Martyr combination lock. We've keyed each lock so that one key, the master key, will unlock them all."

"Who has copies of that key?" Vance asked as he pulled out a notepad.

"I do, Rick does, and so does the school janitor."

"Are all those keys properly secured at night?" Vance asked.

"I keep my keys with me at all times," the principal admitted. "I know Rick does, too. I've made it clear to my vice principal that his job is on the line should anything happen to those keys."

"And the janitor's ring?"

"Locked inside a reinforced steel locker at the end of his shift each night."

"And where's that locker at?" Vance wanted to know. He was scribbling notes like mad.

"Inside the teacher's lounge, next to their lockers."

"Is he the only one who has access to it?"

Principal Reezen dropped a ring of keys on his desk.

"I've also got the key to that locker, if that's what you're asking. Are you suggesting I had something to do with the pendant's disappearance?"

Vance shook his head. "No sir. I'm just collecting facts."

"So, it would appear that the theft occurred sometime after 8:30 p.m. and before 6 a.m. this morning," Captain Nelson said. He sighed and ran a hand through his thinning gray hair. "Very well. Jimmy, Dean, you're coming with me."

"Where are we going?" Jimmy asked fearfully.

"We're going to the station. Detective Samuel-son?"

Vance looked at his boss.

"Captain?"

"Ask your wife to meet us there."

"Excuse me, captain?" Vance sputtered.

"You heard me. Of the three of them, someone must have told someone else. Somebody let something slip that they shouldn't. The pendant has been stolen. Again. Someone must know something."

I saw that Vance had visibly paled.

"Captain, look. I know it looks bad for my wife. However, I have to assure you that she had nothing to do with this."

"I've changed my mind. I'll have someone else call on your wife to bring her in. In fact, it's late. We'll reconvene tomorrow morning. I'll send someone for your wife, Samuelson."

"Great," Vance grumbled. "It ought to be a real hoot around my house tonight."

"Detective?" Captain Nelson called out.

Vance looked up. "Yeah?"

"I'm officially pulling you off this case."

"What?!" Vance sputtered. "Captain, you can't do that! This is my case!"

"And your wife has been implicated, detective. You and I both know that you need to distance yourself until this has all blown over. Do I make myself clear?"

Vance groaned and rubbed his temples.

"I said, do I make myself clear, detective?" Captain Nelson repeated.

"Crystal, sir."

"Good. You are dismissed, Mr. Samuelson. And take Mr. Anderson with you. That will be all."

Without a word, Vance turned on his heel and strode toward the office door. He hooked an arm through mine as he neared, pulling me along with him. Sherlock was already on his feet and anxiously pulling on his leash, ready to leave.

"Dude, I'm sorry," I managed to get out as soon as we pushed open the school doors and hit the night air. "There must be some way they can let you back on the case. You're their best detective!"

"As much as I don't want to admit it, the captain's right," Vance said. "It's a conflict of interest. I can't officially be on the case as long as Tori has been implicated."

Sherlock whined as he looked at the detective. Vance squatted down and ruffled the fur behind Sherlock's ears. A look of resolve appeared on my friend's face. Vance looked up at me and nodded.

"But unofficially? You and I are gonna solve this thing."

A sharp, piercing bark sounded from the lone canine present.

"You, too, pal," Vance added, draping a friendly arm around Sherlock.

"Where do we start?" I asked as we both headed toward the car.

Tori had driven Jillian and Watson back to my

place around an hour ago. As far as I was aware, they were waiting for us there. I unlocked my Jeep and lifted Sherlock into the back seat.

Vance checked his watch, "Shoot. I never realized it was so late."

I checked my watch. Bare skin met my eyes. I forgot I hadn't worn a watch in years, yet the habit was hard to break if anyone uttered the magic phrase what time is it?

"Whatever we're gonna do, it'll have to be tonight," Vance said as he climbed in to my Jeep.

As I pulled out of the school parking lot Vance called their babysitter and asked if she'd be willing to stay even longer, which she was. Apparently, he was planning on breaking the news to Tori about her implication in the case at my house.

Peachy.

This was gonna be a long night. I remembered that none of us had had dinner yet so I placed an order with Sara's Pizza Parlour. I glanced over at Vance as I drove and saw that he was deep in thought. I had to feel bad for the guy. I wouldn't want my wife involved in any type of crime, either. He was probably wondering how he was going to break the news to Tori.

I parked my Jeep next to Jillian's SUV. The lights were on in my house and I could hear some music playing. Looked like Jillian found my CD collection and had chosen some smooth jazz.

Watson met us at the door, barking excitedly.

Sherlock yipped once as he ran up the steps. Tori took one look at her husband and knew—instantly—that something was wrong. Jillian was sitting on the sofa with a beer in her hand. She took one look at us and immediately set her beer down on the coffee table.

"What is it?" Jillian asked. "What's wrong?"

Vance joined his wife on the couch and sighed heavily.

"You're gonna have to tell her sooner or later," I told my friend. "Might as well get it over with."

"You might as well get what over with?" Tori asked as she turned to her husband. "Vance, what are you not telling me?"

"The captain knows about you and that darn pendant," Vance miserably said.

"And how would he know that?" Tori demanded. "You didn't tell him, did you?"

"Tor, I had no choice! I had to admit to my boss that I had been withholding evidence on the case. Do you have any idea how bad that is for a detective?"

"What. Did. You. Tell. Them."

"Tori, I know you're angry. You have every right to be. And, I'm sorry to say, it gets worse."

"How could it get worse, Vance?" Tori wanted to know. Her voice was rising and it didn't take a genius to see that her emotions were starting to show.

"Captain Nelson is sending someone to collect you tomorrow morning."

"What?! Am I being arrested?"

"No," Vance said as he took her hands in his. "They want to ask you questions about how you knew the pendant was real. They've got it in their heads that you let it slip to one of your students and that's how they knew it was worth a lot of money."

"I did no such thing," Tori snapped, pulling her hands free from her husband's. "Why didn't you tell them that?"

"He did tell them that," I added. "Over and over. He protested your innocence so much that they pulled him from the case."

Shocked, Tori looked back at her detective husband.

"They didn't."

"They had no choice," Vance admitted. "I can't fault them for that, babe. The moment you were implicated it became a conflict of interest for me to continue to lead this investigation."

"What am I going to do? I can't go to jail!"

"That's why we're going to solve this," Vance assured her, taking her hands back. "Tonight."

"Tonight? How?"

"We're going to go over everything that is known about the case so far. Four heads are better than one. Perhaps together we can find something that was overlooked?"

"That's your plan for keeping me out of jail?" Tori skeptically asked.

"Do you have a better one?" Vance countered.

"No."

"Okay. Let's get started. Zack, do you have something we can write on? Notebooks, note-pads, etc.?"

I grinned. "I'm a writer. Of course I do."

Fifteen minutes later we were all munching on hot pizza and taking notes on our respective note-books.

"Okay, to get started, let's review what we know. Jimmy Nelson and Dean Rupert learn about the pendant's presence in Egyptian Exhibitions..."

"Jimmy Nelson," Tori muttered. "He was the one that saw I had Googled the pendant. I noticed he was standing there only I don't know how long he was looking. Oh, good God. I am responsible for this."

"You didn't force those boys to steal the neck-lace," Jillian reminded her. "It's not your fault, Tori."

"Tweedle Dee and Tweedle Dum hatch a plan to steal the necklace," Vance continued as he made a few notes in his notebook. "They figured they'd also get a good chuckle out of this whole scheme by making it look like the mummy woke up from the dead, swiped the pendant, and wandered off.

"Now this next part is speculation," Vance said as he pulled his small, official police notebook from his back pocket. "We're guessing that later that night Jimmy went back to the school in an attempt to sneak the pendant off the school's campus, only his presence was discovered by Sherlock. We tracked him through the school to the band room only to lose him when he threw a chair through the window. Consequently, that's what cut up his hands. Zack, remember the blood on his mummy costume? It was from the wounds he sustained trying to get through the broken window as fast as possible."

"So, at this point, the necklace is still at the school, right?" I asked.

"Pendant," Tori corrected.

"Whatever," I grumped.

"Yes," Vance answered. "People were being searched as they left the school. They knew that they wouldn't be able to smuggle the pendant out of the school. Not without being caught. I can only assume it was at this time both boys realized they had bitten off more than they could chew. So now the question is, what do they do with the pendant? By his own admission the pendant is in Jimmy's locker. Now what does he do with it? They dare not show it to anyone. The whole town was talking about the mummy and the theft."

"I would say that it was right about then that the boys continue to fuel the rumor that the mummy had indeed come back to life and was now terrorizing the town," I added.

Zack nodded. "Right. These two hooligans incite panic by appearing in various places around town, but only in locations where they can make a clean getaway."

"I almost had the twerp," I recalled. "I chased him from Gary's Grocery all the way to the high school."

"Thus proving we were dealing with high school kids," Vance confirmed. "Not very bright kids at that. But, it worked to our advantage."

"How?" Tori asked.

"Because they kept showing off," Vance told her. He looked up at me and nodded. "They wanted to show that they were smarter than everyone else and keep the town paralyzed with fear."

"I think they relished the attention," Jillian softly added.

"Of that, I have no doubt," Vance said, giving Jillian a nod of his head. "So what do they do? They wait until it starts to get dark. They get into costume and sneak into the maze using that tiny trail that could barely be called a road."

"But how did they get a car in there without it being heard?" Jillian asked. "You know as well as I do that it's very quiet out in that field. An engine would be easily heard."

"That's one of the things we need to figure out," Vance admitted. "I'll add it to my list."

As if we were all in a class listening to a professor give a lecture, the three of us jotted the same thing down in our own respective notebooks.

"Now, this is where it starts to get good," Vance said, rubbing his hands together. "Zack and I catch Jimmy and Dean in the maze. Sherlock IDs Jimmy from the school and he finally confesses to master-minding the whole operation. Jimmy admits that he and Dean stole the pendant, and the mummy, and stashed the pendant in his locker."

"Number 151," Vance recalled, glancing at his notebook. "Sherlock led us straight to his locker a few days after the crime took place. Now, I will admit that I'm curious. Did he take us to the locker because he smelled marijuana or was it because he somehow knew the pendant was in that locker?"

"I'd have to go with the latter explanation," I decided. "When we left that locker, Sherlock kept looking back at it. He was reluctant to leave, as if he were trying to tell us that we were missing something. I think the pendant was still in the locker at that time."

Vance nodded. "I would agree. So, now that we caught the perpetrators, we're told where the pendant had been stashed, only guess what? The pendant wasn't there."

"Do you believe the boys when they said they didn't know where it went?" Tori asked.

Vance shrugged. "It's hard to say."

"I'll say it," I announced. "I happened to be looking straight at Jimmy when the principal announced there was nothing in the locker. The look on the kid's face was priceless. There was someone who truly thought the pendant was in that locker. Both of them did."

"So how was it stolen?" Tori asked. "How did

someone else figure out where the pendant was?"

Vance shrugged and held up his hands in an I-don't-know gesture. He picked up his notebook and added some more notes. The rest of us did the same. Vance finished writing and looked up at us.

"Alright, that's two things for the list. Does anyone else have anything to add?"

I cleared my throat. "I'll say. You're forgetting about Ammar Fadil."

Vance snapped his fingers. "You're right. I totally forgot about him. Okay, we also need to figure out how it's humanly possible to turn a body into a mummified person in less than a day."

"It's not," Tori vowed. "No matter how you look at it, you can't rush the laws of physics. Certain things take a very specific amount of time to accomplish. There's simply no way for a body to become mummified in such a short amount of time."

"Then how?" Vance demanded. "You tell me how it's possible."

I made a 'T' out of my hands and held them up for everyone to see.

"Ok, wait a minute. Let's look at this logically. If what Tori says is true, and I'm inclined to believe her since we heard Dr. Tarik say the very same thing a few days ago, a human corpse takes somewhere around 35-70 days to become a mummy. There are no shortcuts, so that can only mean it was done by the usual way."

"But there wasn't enough time!" Vance protested. "We saw the assistant on the night of the heist, remember? That was only a few days ago."

"That's right," I confirmed. "That would mean that the body isn't Ammar Fadil."

"Dr. Tarik would disagree with you," Vance pointed out. "As would modern science. While we don't yet have the complete results from the lab, thus far the DNA recovered from the mummified body is pointing to one person: the assistant. It has to be Ammar Fadil."

"What if it isn't?" I asked, warming up. "Could it be someone else? You said it yourself. The DNA analysis hasn't been completed. Preliminary results can still be wrong."

"Look, Zack," Vance said, as he set the small notebook down and reached for his beer, "you can't fool a DNA test. The only way that body couldn't be Ammar Fadil was if ... was if..."

"...if he had a twin?" Jillian quietly suggested. "Is that what you were going to say, Vance?"

"I was going to suggest another family member, like his father," I said, "but a twin would work. Do twins have the same DNA?"

"I believe I can answer that," Tori said, raising a hand. "I've done genetic studies before. A typical person has about a hundred new mutations in their DNA. Spread that out over six million base pairs and you're looking for a needle in a haystack. Give it enough time and someone, somewhere, might be able to come up with a way for scientists to be able to tell identical twins' DNA apart. To answer your question, Zack, technically no, but as far as forensic science is concerned, yes. There is no way to tell the DNA apart. Not yet, anyway."

"So what are you saying?" I asked, looking around the room. "Are you telling me that, forensically speaking, the mummified body could be Ammar's twin? Then what happened to Ammar?"

Vance was silent as he considered. He then pulled his cell from his pocket, placed a call, quickly terminated said call, and then looked over at Tori.

"I can't call the station about this. I'm off the case. That would have been bad. Tor, tell me something. Last year, at Christmas. What was the name of your friend we ran into at the mall in Medford?"

"Connie?"

"No, not Connie. She was short, had black hair, and had a tattoo on her right shoulder."

"Oh. Susan? What about her?"

"What's her last name?" Vance asked. He had returned his attention to his phone and was scrolling through the many numbers in his phone's address book.

"Williams. You want to call Susan? Why?"

"Not Susan but her husband, Jeremy. I know I've got them in my address book but I must not have punched in their last name. I can't find them anywhere."

"That's because Susan's husband is Jessie," Tori pointed out.

"Right. Jessie."

"What do you want to talk to Jessie Williams for?"

Vance found the entry and tapped the number. Once it was ringing, he finally looked up at Tori.

"Because Jessie Williams works at the FBI. He owes me a favor. It's time to collect."

"You've got friends in the FBI?" I asked, impressed. "Not bad, pal. Not bad at all."

"He's ... hello? I'd like to speak to special agent Jessie Williams, please. That's right, he's out of the Medford, Oregon, office. Hmm? What's that? Oh. Detective Vance Samuelson, Pomme Valley Police Department. Yes, ma'am. I'm in Oregon, too. Thank you. I'll wait."

"I thought you had a direct number to him?" Tori asked.

"That makes two of us," Vance grumbled. "The last time I did this I got straight through to him. They must have changed their phone system. Maybe they changed their ... hello? Jessie? It's Vance Samuelson, PVPD. How's it goin', buddy? Listen, I need to call in that favor you owe me. I need a background check for one Ammar Fadil. He's an assistant curator at a traveling show called Egyptian Exhibitions. I need to know about Ammar's family. Brothers, sisters, aunts, uncles, etc. I need to know if there's any connection to PV. You will? That's great. Thanks, pal. Yes, that's still my cell number. I look forward to your call. Thanks again." Vance hung up and looked at each of us. "We should have some answers shortly."

"If it turns out Ammar has a twin," I slowly began, "what does that tell us? Who killed his brother? How did he end up in a corn field?"

"I would say that someone definitely went to a lot of trouble to get that necklace," Vance mused. He polished off his beer and leaned back on the couch.

"If I didn't know any better," I said as I finished my own beer, "I'd say those two punks messed up someone else's plans."

Vance looked at me, his eyes opening wide.

"Say that again, Zack."

"What? The part about the kids messing up someone else's plans?"

"Yeah. That's it. I think you hit the nail on the head. In fact, it makes total sense. I think I've got this figured out."

"We're all ears, pal," I told my friend.

Jillian placed her hand over mine. A split second later Watson jumped up onto the couch with us and settled herself directly between me and Jillian. She turned to regard Jillian with an expression that almost said, Behave yourself around my daddy. I almost choked.

Vance regarded Watson with a bemused expression on his face. "I'm gonna go grab another beer. Do you mind?"

I shook my head. "Help yourself."

"I think someone is jealous," Vance decided, once he returned.

"She's a dog," I pointed out. "How could a dog be jealous?"

Jillian stroked the silky fur on the back of Watson's neck.

"Don't you worry about your daddy," Jillian assured the little corgi. "I would never hurt him."

Watson turned to gaze up into Jillian's eyes. She licked her hand in response. I also noticed that she had sighed happily, indicating she wasn't planning on going anywhere anytime soon.

"As I was saying," Vance said, trying again, "I have a theory. I think what we have here are two separate crimes, only the first happened before the second could be played out."

"You're thinking someone has been planning on stealing the pendant for quite some time now," I guessed.

"Nothing screams out premeditation like mummifying a body," Vance agreed.

"I want to hear Vance's theory," Jillian announced. "All of it, from start to finish."

Vance took another pull on his beer, managed to close his mouth before the belch could escape, and then pulled his notebooks closer.

"Okay, here goes. I'm thinking our friend Ammar, who is employed by an organization responsible for setting up a mobile display of Egyptian artifacts, decided he was tired of making peanuts. My guess is that he somehow learned about the plan to transport that pendant across the United States by being presented as just another trinket in a show that has nothing but replicas of the real thing."

"With you so far," I said. Jillian promptly shushed me.

"Now, Ammar starts making plans. He…"

"How could he have possibly made plans that far ahead to steal Nekhbet's Pendant from PV?" Tori asked, perplexed. "Their visit here was a last minute decision. At least that's what Dr. Tarik told me."

"Let's assume what you say is true," Vance told his wife. "Let's say the mastermind behind all of this didn't know about this stop in PV. In fact I'm willing to bet he didn't have a clue. However, with that being said, I'd say Ammar discovered he had the perfect opportunity to pull it off."

"Here in PV?" I skeptically asked. "How?"

"Think about it," Vance urged me. "They knew they were going to pull off this robbery of the necklace."

"Pendant," Tori corrected.

Vance grinned and shook his head.

"Pendant. Whatever. They knew it was going to be difficult to pull off the heist in a big-name city. Pomme Valley presented too tempting of a locale to pass up. So Ammar began preparations to steal the pendant, only…"

"Someone beat him to it," Jillian added. She nodded her head. "That's impressive, Vance."

"Oh, don't praise him," Tori moaned. "His head's already big enough."

"I heard that," Vance said, not bothering to look up from his notes. "Continuing on. Now Ammar is in trouble. All his carefully laid out plans are for naught. After months of planning, he ended up with not a darn thing."

"How does this help us?" I asked. "Where does that leave us?"

"I'm getting to it," Vance answered. "Keep your panties on. Now. Let's switch gears for just a moment to young Mr. Nelson and his counterpart, Dean Rupert. Jimmy Nelson just happens to discover that one of the items in the Egyptian show setting up in the school happens to be worth lots of money. What's a young teenager to do when tempted with that much money?"

"Not all high school kids think like that," Tori scolded, throwing her husband a frown.

"But they should still know right from wrong," I pointed out. "Nobody held a gun to their heads and forced them to steal the necklace."

"Pendant," Tori corrected.

"Whatever," I grinned.

"Thanks, Zack," Vance said. "That's the point I was trying to make. Kids should know when NOT to make a bad decision. Anyway, back to the point. Two kids are tempted enough to do something about it. So they hatch a plan to steal the pendant," Vance threw a look at Tori, who returned his look with a grin. "They make it look like a mummy is the culprit and have a little fun terrorizing the town in the process."

"Only the boys don't have the pendant," Tori reminded him.

Vance tapped his small notebook, "It's next on my list. So, the boys pull off the heist, stash the loot in one of their lockers, and then try to figure out what to do with it now that they've got it. Trying to fence stolen goods isn't as easy as the movies make it look."

"But now someone else has the pendant," Jillian said.

Vance nodded. "Right. Somehow one of those boys let it slip to someone else that they were the ones who pulled off the heist. Somehow someone else figured it out."

"Let's say someone did," I said, drawing everyone's attention. "How would they know where to find the pendant? How would they even know where to look?"

"It's not too hard to figure out that the first place to look for stolen goods, if you suspected a student, would be their locker. Someone managed to open Jimmy's locker, search through it undetected, take the pendant, and then put everything back the way it was."

"The only other person to do that would be Ammar," I pointed out. "Do you think he has the fortitude to pull that off?"

Jillian leaned forward to whisper in my ear.

"Nice word, Zachary. And I do, by the way. It sounds like he's been making these plans for a while."

CASE OF THE FLEET-FOOTED MUMMY

I patted her hand, "True."

Watson woofed a warning. Jillian smiled, scratched behind the corgi's ears, and settled back against the sofa. Watson returned to her nap.

"Zack, you can't possibly think that Ammar is innocent, can you?" Vance sputtered. "I mean, aren't you the writer? Isn't that supposed to mean you have an active imagination?"

"I never said I was a mystery writer," I pointed out.

"What type of writer are you?" Tori asked. "I don't think I've ever heard you say which genre you write in. I'll have to look up some of your books."

Uh-oh! I needed a subject change and I needed one now! Thankfully I was saved by an incoming call on Vance's cell.

"Detective Samuelson. Hey, Jeremy. Thanks for calling me back. I..."

"His name is Jessie!" Tori hissed at him.

"Jessie. Sorry 'bout that. It's been a long day. What do you have for me? Okay ... uh huh. Wow, really? Talk about an unlucky family. How long ago? Okay. I ... what? He did? I'll be damned. That's definitely good news for me. Okay, Jessie. Thank you very much."

Vance pocketed his cell and looked at the three of us. He held up a finger—signaling us to wait —and picked up his notebook. He began writing furiously. For two solid minutes Vance mumbled to himself and transferred his thoughts to paper.

219

Tori finally cleared her throat.

"Care to share? We're all dying over here."

"Just a minute," Vance mumbled as he hastily scribbled notes down on his pad. Finished, he looked up. "Okay, Jessie had a veritable treasure trove of information. Get this. Ammar Fadil comes from a large family. A large unlucky family."

"Unlucky in what way?" I asked.

"Both his brother and his father are missing."

"Well, now we know he has a brother," I said.

"Jessie says that the Fadil family had ten children. He didn't know if any of them were twins but when you have that many kids, I'd say there would be a high chance of the family having one set. Maybe two."

"You said a brother and the father are missing," Tori reminded him. "What happened? Did he say?"

"The father disappeared while looking for the missing son," Vance said, reading his notes. "When the son went missing, the father took it upon himself to look for him since the local police weren't much help."

"The police weren't much help?" I repeated, amazed. "Since when? Isn't it their job?"

"Police departments in other countries might not be as thorough as we are here in the States," Vance told me.

"How long ago did the brother disappear?" Jillian asked.

Vance consulted his notes.

"Two months."

"Two months?" Tori repeated, growing excited. "That time frame would fit with how long it'd take to turn a body into a mummy! And wow, I really shouldn't get that excited about that. Sorry."

Jillian stifled a giggle. Sherlock, who had been curled up by my feet, suddenly rose, stretched, and then jumped onto the couch to settle on the other side of Jillian. Within moments, the tricolor corgi had resumed his nap.

"The mummified body has gotta be Ammar's brother," Vance continued after he smiled at the corgis. "The time frame fits the facts."

"What nationality is the Fadil family?" I asked.

"Egyptian," Vance said. "Why?"

"Does the family still live in Egypt?"

Vance nodded. "Cairo. What about it?"

"How did they get a mummified body all the way from Cairo to here?" I asked. "It's not like PV was the first stop on their American tour. How did they conceal the body for that long?"

"That's an easy one," Tori said as she looked my way. "They are already taking around an Egyptian sarcophagus with them. They've already got one authentic mummy. I'd say that either that sarcophagus has a false bottom or else Ammar was the one responsible for caring for the real mummy. If he was the only person who was opening and closing that casket then he'd be able to conceal the fact that Egyptian Exhibitions was carrying around not one but two mummies."

Vance's cell rang.

"Hello? Oh, hey, Jessie. What's up? He what? Are you sure it's him? Okay, thanks for letting me know. Yeah, it does help my investigation. Thanks again."

"What?" I prompted. "What was that all about?"

"Jessie wanted to let me know he came across an Egyptian police report. He didn't know why it wasn't tied to the report on the rest of the family. Ammar's father was found dead last month."

"Oh, that poor family," Jillian softly. "I feel bad for the mother."

"You said something about good news," I remembered. "What was that all about?"

Vance snapped his fingers.

"Thanks for reminding me!" He turned to Tori and took her hands in his. "What would you say if I told you that you were not responsible for bringing Egyptian Exhibitions to PV?"

"But I was!" Tori protested. "I alone sent them daily emails. I alone nagged them until they finally agreed to listen to my petition. Trust me, I'm the reason they stopped in PV."

"Except you weren't," Vance argued. "Jessie was able to access the Fadil family's phone records. Guess what? Someone in that family has been in touch with someone here in the United States."

"Not surprising," I decided. "Why is that good

news?"

"Because the number that was dialed was located here in Oregon and it was within the last month."

My eyebrows shot up.

"Umm, which part?" I asked, already knowing the answer.

"Pomme Valley," Vance proudly announced. "Someone in the Fadil family, and I don't think it takes a rocket scientist to figure out it was Ammar, had called a PV number several times."

"Do we know who it was?" Tori asked, growing excited once more.

Vance nodded. "We do. It's a cell phone number and it is currently registered to one Victor Preston."

I shrugged. "Does anyone know who that is? I don't."

"Nor do I," Jillian admitted.

"Have either of you heard of the Square L convenience store?" Vance asked.

All of us were nodding.

"Sure," I said. "It's in the grocery store parking lot."

"The Square L is Preston's store."

"That's a wee bit on the suspicious side," I decided.

"Oh, it gets better," Vance assured me. He flipped a few pages in his notebook and turned it around so that we could see the chicken scratch he called handwriting. He excitedly tapped the page.

"Guess who has a part time job at that store?"

"Who?" I asked.

"Dean Rupert," Vance smugly said.

TEN

Surprised, I looked around the room. Tori and Jillian had shocked looks on their faces, too. Sherlock woke up and looked at me. Right about then I remembered that for the last two or three days Sherlock had barked at the little convenience store every time I had driven by it.

I shook my head in amazement. Sherlock had done it again. How the heck had he known shady things were afoot at the Square L?

"So one of the boys works there?" I asked. "You think that's how this Victor person figured out one of his employees had robbed the school?"

Vance nodded. "Yes. Boys will be boys. What do you want to bet that they were overheard bragging about the theft? Or maybe they were arguing because they couldn't find a way to safely sell the necklace without alerting every Tom, Dick, and Harry. It doesn't matter. What does matter is we now have a lead!"

"Why haven't you called this in?" Tori demanded. "I'm due to be arrested tomorrow morning!"

"You're being called in for questioning," Vance clarified. "You're not being arrested. Umm, at least I don't think you are."

Tori's expression soured.

"That's comforting. Answer the question. Why haven't you called this in? If this will give the police someone else to chase after, why haven't you done it? Words cannot begin to describe how much I don't want to go to the station tomorrow morning."

"I can't call this in until we get that little something called proof," Vance explained, albeit a tad sarcastically.

"Can't you show them what you've found?" Jillian asked. She pointed at Vance's notebooks. "Can't you tell them you were given some new leads and they've ... what's the phrase? Panned out?"

"I've been pulled from the case," Vance reminded everyone. "I can't go back to my captain unless I have definitive proof that Victor Preston is actively involved."

"And how are you planning on accomplishing that?" I asked.

Vance stood, unholstered his weapon, checked the clip, and then slid the gun back into its place under his left shoulder.

"I'm going over there to check out the store. Poke around a little."

Tori automatically looked over at the closest clock. It was past 8 p.m. She rose to her feet and collected her purse and jacket.

"I'll go with you. I can call..."

"Like hell you will!" Vance snapped. "Seriously, Tor? This is not some random visit to the grocery store. People have died here. Do you really think I'll let you step into harm's way? It's out of the question. Stay put."

Tori frowned and crossed her arms over her chest.

"Stay put? What am I, a dog?"

Two canine heads popped up, much like how a prairie dog would stick his head up out of his burrow. I winced. That was one word that both Sherlock and Watson knew well. Dog. The slightest mention of that word would have both corgis checking the immediate surroundings to see if another dog had somehow appeared in their territory.

Tori patted both corgis on their heads.

"I'm sorry. Poor choice of words. Go back to sleep." Tori looked up at her husband. "As for you, mister..."

Vance held up his hands, signaling a surrender.

"Sorry, that's not what I meant. However, you will be staying here. Zack, would you care to join me?"

I eyeballed the weapon dangling from Vance's shoulder holster just before it was concealed under his jacket.

"I'm not sure I should. Isn't this a police matter?"

"It is, and I'm pretty sure we're not going to find anything, but I would like someone there who has my back."

"But I don't," I pointed out. "I don't have a gun."

Vance pulled up his right pants leg, revealing a snub-nosed revolver nestled in an ankle holster. He nearly had it unbuckled before I came to my senses. He had squatted down so that he could access the smaller gun. I hooked an arm under his shoulder and pulled him to his feet.

"I didn't say I wanted a gun," I clarified, "only that I didn't have one. Do you really think that's necessary?"

"Ammar's brother has been murdered," Vance reminded me. "A priceless piece of ugly Egyptian jewelry has been stolen. Would you really put it past him to not try and defend himself if he thinks he's in danger?"

"That's gotta be why Sherlock kept barking at that store," I said, as I reached for my ASU sweatshirt.

Vance had just zipped up his jacket when he paused.

"What was that? Did you say that Sherlock has been barking at the Square L?"

I nodded. "Yeah. For the past couple of days. Every time I drove by, he'd bark his fool head off at it. I never could figure out why."

"And that's how he behaved when he barked at the pet store several months ago, wasn't it?" Vance recalled. "When that glass tiger went missing. Do you remember it?"

"How could I forget it?" I asked. "I was the one being accused of theft and murder that time around. It's not something I'm going to be forgetting any time soon."

Vance whistled. "Wow, you sure do hold a grudge, don't you? What I meant was, we were looking for that tiger. You said Sherlock kept barking at the store. Clearly, he wanted you to check it out. He must be doing the same thing here. Damn, Zack. I wish you would've told me sooner."

"Told you what?" I asked. "That Sherlock barked at something? Dude, I'd be calling you up all the time."

Vance kissed his wife and headed toward the door. I moved to follow Vance. I made it about three steps before Sherlock caught up with me. Watson tried to follow, but thankfully Jillian caught the little female corgi before she could jump down from the couch. The look Watson gave Jillian was priceless. I never knew that pets—especially dogs—could convey so much emotion in their faces. Watson's look to Jillian clearly said, mind your own business.

I clipped a leash onto Sherlock's collar, "Let's go, buddy. We've got a bad guy to find."

Sherlock barked excitedly. Watson let out an exasperated whine. Both corgis looked at each other and I swear Sherlock gave his pack mate a smirk.

"You be careful," Jillian said as she rose to her feet. She waggled a finger at Vance. "Don't you dare put him in harm's way. If you do, then you'll have to answer to me; is that understood?"

"And me," Tori added as she stood.

Vance stared at the two women and shook his head.

"Oh, sure, worry about him and not me, huh? Don't worry, dear. I'm sure I'll be fine. Man, I can feel the love in this room."

Before I knew what I was doing, I was surprising myself by giving Jillian a hug and a kiss on the cheek before I followed Vance outside. Just as I was closing the door, I heard hushed, excited chattering and a few giggles. Let them talk. I didn't care. I was actually feeling pretty good, regardless of the fact that there was a chance I could be putting myself and Sherlock in danger.

I glanced over at Vance. He had started toward his Oldsmobile sedan when he stopped and looked at my Jeep.

"Let's take yours."

"Why?" I asked.

"Because I don't want mine to get shot up, okay? Now let's go!"

I remained rooted to the spot, arm outstretched and hand firmly gripping the door handle. I stared at my friend. If that was a joke, then that was some seriously bad timing.

"Relax a little, would you?" Vance teased. "I was joking."

"Hilarious, dude."

Vance laughed as we drove down my driveway.

"So how many times has Sherlock barked at the Square L?" Vance wanted to know.

"Let's see. Several times yesterday, once the day before, and once the day before that."

"And prior to that?"

I shrugged. "I hadn't really noticed. I don't think he had at all."

"You do realize that coincides with the disappearance of the necklace from Jimmy's locker, don't you?"

"Well, yeah. Now I do."

I turned on the radio and set it to an oldies station. The Beach Boys were singing about good vibrations. Vance hit the channel up button, forcing my satellite radio to begin playing a country music song. I frowned and set the radio back to my oldies station.

"You're not Jillian, so I can threaten you with breaking off your fingers if you do that again."

Vance laughed. "You don't like country music?"

"Not one bit of it," I admitted. "I mean, did you listen to the lyrics of that last song? The band was singing about someone having to die! How crude is that? I'll stick with my golden oldies, thank you very much."

"So you'd rather listen to old fogey music, is that it?" Vance asked, incredulous.

"I hate to break it to you, pal, but you and I

are really close in age. Not to mention that these songs were popular when we were both kids."

"Thereby insinuating we're both old farts. Nice, Zack. Do me a favor and don't ever talk like that around Tori."

"Why?"

"Because if I start dropping hints that I'm feeling old, then one of two things is going to start happening. Either she'll force me to get more exercise, which I think I'm doing pretty good there, or she could ... and this part scares the heck out of me, force me to change my diet. I'll be honest with you. The last thing I want to do is cut out red meat, or bread, or chips, or ... or..."

"Beer?" I suggested.

Vance shuddered. "Not even funny. Life without beer. Oh, the horrors."

I grinned at him just as we came around the bend and saw the lights on at Gary's Grocery and its huge parking lot. There, on the northeastern corner of the parking lot was the Square L. There were also, I noticed with surprise, several cars parked at three of the four pumps. I pointed at the convenience store. There were also at least half a dozen people peering in through the windows.

The store was dark.

"It's closed?" Vance asked, surprised. He glanced at his watch. "It's not even 8:30. What is he doing closed?"

"This doesn't bode well," I decided.

I pulled the Jeep into the parking space closest

to the door. Vance was out the door before I could bring the Jeep to a stop. I started to get out when Vance turned to look at me and pointed at the car. He wanted me to stay put, too. I was halfway tempted to bark at him. It'd be my luck Sherlock would think a dog was in the car with him and I'd receive a bite for my troubles.

I could see Vance pulling out his badge and talking to a few of the people wandering aimlessly up and down the sidewalk just outside the store. He then walked up to the locked front door, jiggled the handle, then cupped his hands around his eyes and tried to look inside the store. It was too dark to see anything.

Vance looked straight back at me, held up an open hand—palm facing me—and gave me my second doggie command of the day. Wait. I watched him disappear around the back of the store. A few minutes later he reemerged on the other side, having completely circled the store, presumably looking for a way to get in. He looked back at me and waved me over.

"Come on, Sherlock. I think we're on."

Amidst a chorus of 'what a cute dog!' comments, Sherlock and I approached the darkened store.

"Anything?" I asked.

Vance shook his head no.

"I think we're too late. I think Victor has cut out of town. And why not? With that necklace he could buy himself a whole fleet of stores in a new town. Dammit!"

I felt Sherlock pull on his leash. Apparently, he wanted to follow in Vance's footsteps and make a complete circuit of the place. He barked and pulled on the leash again.

"What's he doing?" Vance asked.

I noticed my detective friend had his cell phone in his hand, as though he was trying to convince himself to phone Captain Nelson and let him know what he had learned thus far. However, as he had so eloquently stated not so long ago, it would look exceedingly bad for him if he couldn't back up any of his story without having a shred of tangible proof.

"I think Sherlock wants to look around. Should I let him?"

Vance looked down at his cell and slid it back into a pocket.

"What the heck. At this point it couldn't hurt. Maybe he can find something."

I gave Sherlock some leash and let him wander around the perimeter of the building. We got as far as the back door, which was what Victor Preston must have used to receive his deliveries, when Sherlock paused. He yipped once, pulled me over to the back door with as much grace as a farmer using an ox to plow a field, and looked pointedly at the door.

"I've already tried it," Vance announced, coming up behind me. "It's locked."

"You heard him, Sherlock," I told the corgi,

pulling on his leash so we could keep circling the store. "Yes, you found a way inside, but we can't get in there. Come on. Let's keep searching."

Sherlock refused to budge. He looked up at me, whined, and then looked back at the door. He let out a short, high-pitched yip of frustration.

"What's wrong with him?" Vance asked.

"I'm not sure. He doesn't want to leave. The last time he did this was back at the school, when we were searching the locker. I'm pretty sure the pendant was in that locker when we searched it. If I didn't know any better, I'd say there's something here that we're both missing."

"Like what?" Vance wanted to know. "I've tried the door. It's locked." The detective grabbed the door handle and gave it a little jiggle. "See? It ... I'll be a monkey's uncle."

I was about to ask what the problem was when Vance held a finger to his lips and pointed down at the bottom of the door. I looked down. The door had moved! It must not have closed all the way, indicating our friend Mr. Preston had left in a hurry.

Vance paused, placed his ear up against the door, and then grunted with surprise. He looked down at the bottom of the door as he eased it open another few inches. His gun suddenly appeared in his hand.

"Zack, get Sherlock out of here. Now!"

He didn't need to ask me twice. I scooped up Sherlock in my arms and retreated to the safety of the parking lot where there was more light. And witnesses.

"What is it? What's the matter?"

"There's someone in there!" Vance reported. He grasped the door handle and pulled. The door swung open. "That's why Sherlock led us to this door. He must have heard something in the store! Wait here!"

From nearly fifty feet away Sherlock and I watched as Vance chambered a round into his gun and ducked into the store. Less than ten seconds later Vance's head poked out of the door.

"Zack! Get over here! You're not gonna believe this."

Sherlock and I hurried over to the door and cautiously stepped inside. I could see Vance standing on a chair, looking into the manager's tiny office through the only window it had. He motioned me over and stepped off the chair.

"Have a look for yourself."

I looked through the window. Someone was inside, tied, and gagged. He was struggling furiously with his bonds, but wasn't making any leeway with them. He had yet to see either of us staring at him through the office's tiny window.

"Who's that?" I asked. "Is it Victor Preston?"

Vance stared at me in disbelief.

"Zack, that's Ammar Fadil!"

"What?!"

I stepped up onto the chair again for a second look. That's what threw me. The last time I had seen our friend Mr. Fadil he was wearing the same dark green shirt and khaki pants that the Egyptian Exhibitions' uniformed staff wore. This time his clothing consisted of a dark blue turtle-neck sweater, black trousers, and a pair of black sneakers.

I must have made some noise as I stepped up onto the chair because this time Ammar was looking straight at me. His eyes pleaded for help. I nodded and stepped down.

"He knows we're here," I told Vance.

"He knows you are here," Vance corrected. "I knew I heard something."

"Oh, please," I scoffed. "You're going to tell me that you really did hear Ammar making some noise? Calling for help? You don't expect me to buy that, do you? You were just looking for some pretense to enter the building."

"I really did hear him," Vance insisted. "That's when I looked at the door and wondered if I could kick it in, but didn't have to. The door hadn't quite shut all the way, almost like whoever was leaving had left in a hurry. Let's go let our new friend out, shall we?"

We tried the lock to the office door. It wouldn't open. Vance gripped either side of the door frame and kicked the door open. Ammar's look of relief switched to terror when he saw Vance and saw the badge on his belt. He looked accusingly back at me.

"Hey, he's the one who heard you," I told the unfortunate man. "He was already with me when you saw me."

Vance produced a pocket knife and cut the ropes holding Ammar's gag in place.

"Well?" Ammar demanded. "Aren't you going to cut me loose?"

Vance pulled out his cell and, with a broad smile on his face, dialed a number from memory.

"Not yet, pal," Vance said. "I know a few people who have got to see this."

* * *

"I'm telling you again that I had nothing to do with this!" Ammar Fadil protested. "I am the victim here; do you not understand?"

We were sitting in one of the larger conference rooms down at the police station since the standard interrogation room wouldn't hold all the people who were present. Captain Nelson, Vance, Dr. Tarik, half a dozen police officers I didn't know, the district attorney, and even the mayor had wanted to witness the interrogation. I think the moral of the story here is to not try and sully a small town's name. Everyone who was anyone wanted to make sure that the perpetrator was brought to justice.

Captain Nelson looked over at Vance and inclined his head. Vance smiled, as did I. That one simple nod had just allowed Vance back on the case.

"We know, Mr. Fadil."

"You know what?" Ammar Fadil asked, feigning ignorance.

"We know all about your plan."

"What plan? I am the victim here! I was the one who was kidnapped and held against my will! Why aren't you looking for that deplorable store owner?"

"And who would that be?" Vance calmly asked, as if he was bored out of his skull with this interrogation.

"Victor Preston! He's the one that set everything up! He's the one who stole the pendant!"

"Is that so?" Vance asked. He glanced around the room for effect. "Why don't you tell us what you know and then I'll let you know which parts you're lying about."

Several beads of sweat had started trickling down Ammar's face. He swallowed nervously, faked a coughing fit, and when that failed to generate the slightest bit of sympathy, he sighed. He placed both hands on the table and linked his fingers together.

"Could I trouble you for a glass of water?"

Vance shrugged. "Sure. I wouldn't want your mouth to go dry when you're doing such a fantastic job of trying to blow smoke at us."

Once a pitcher of water and a glass had been added to the table, Ammar looked despairingly around the room.

"You can try to stall for time all you want," Vance told the formerly missing assistant, "but all it's doing is giving us more time to finalize all the charges we will be leveling against you. Do you want to help yourself? I would advise you to come clean."

"But I don't know anything!" Ammar whined.

"Fine. We'll do it my way. First, let's talk about your family."

"What about my family?" Ammar asked, startled.

"We know the mummified body is your brother's."

All the color drained out of Ammar's face.

"We know your father was found dead last month."

Ammar hastily poured himself another glass of water and gulped it down.

"It'll only be a matter of time before we pin his murder back on you," Vance casually added. "What happened, Mr. Fadil? Did your father learn you had killed your brother? Were you forced to kill your father, too?"

Ammar was silent as he stared straight ahead.

"And then you turned your brother into a mummy," Vance said. "What kind of sick, twisted, sadistic son of a bitch would do that to his own brother?"

"You know nothing," Ammar sneered, dropping his innocent act.

"So how'd you get your brother's body into the States? Did you conceal him with the real mummy?"

"American customs laws are pathetic and

weak," Ammar snapped. "You can get anything into this country if you know the right people."

"We'll be sure to pass that along," Captain Nelson said, breaking his silence. "I'm sure you just made a number of high-ranking officials very concerned. They are going to want to talk to you. Then again, you shouldn't worry. I'm sure your schedule has just opened up for the foreseeable future."

"I gotta hand it to you, pal," Vance continued as he consulted his notes, "that was one very intricate plan you hatched. Too bad it didn't work."

"Kids," Ammar softly muttered.

Everyone in the room leaned forward.

"What was that?" Vance asked.

"Two years of planning," Ammar said, bitterly. "Two years of my life ... wasted. Everything was going to plan. We were set to spring the trap that night, only..."

"Only the boys beat you to it," Vance finished for him. "They ... Zack? What is it? Why do you have your hand up? This isn't school."

I hastily lowered my arm.

"Can I ask something really quick?"

An entire roomful of people turned to look at me as though I had no business being there. Well, let's be honest. I really didn't. I think the only reason I was allowed to attend the interrogation was that the captain was a huge fan of Sherlock's.

"Make it quick, Zack."

"Did you catch what he just said?"

"What part?" Vance wanted to know.

"He said 'we'. That means he had a partner."

Surprised, Vance turned back to Ammar. By this time Ammar was scowling. One by one everyone turned their attention to the lone man sitting on the opposite side of the table. Then, in unison, everyone turned to look at Dr. Tarik.

"Don't look at me," Dr. Tarik hastily exclaimed. "I had no knowledge of any of this."

"Mr. Anderson brings up a very good point," Captain Nelson announced. "We know it isn't Dr. Tarik. Identify your partner, Mr. Fadil."

"Go to hell," Ammar sneered.

"It's no big mystery," Vance told his boss. "It's Victor Preston. Ammar has been in contact with him."

"Victor Preston?" the captain repeated. "Why do I know that name?"

"He owns the Square L by the grocery store," Vance answered.

Captain Nelson shook his head. "No, that's not it. I know that name. I've seen it before."

A quick background check gave us the answer. Turned out our friend Victor Preston had a rap sheet. He had even done time for aggravated assault and attempted robbery.

Captain Nelson skimmed the report.

"Thought so. I knew I had heard of him. He's involved in this? Bring him in."

"Looks like he's skipped town, Captain," Vance reluctantly said.

"Are we thinking this is the mastermind behind the heist at the school?"

Vance shook his head. "No, sir. The mastermind you're referring to is your grandson. Ammar had been planning on swiping that vulture thing for quite some time, only Jimmy beat him to it."

"So, where is Mr. Preston now?"

Vance shrugged. "Unknown. We think he left town in a hurry. We checked the store and we checked his house. The store safe was emptied and the house looks as though a tornado hit it. Looks like he was anxious to leave town."

"And the necklace?" Captain Nelson asked. "He has it, doesn't he?"

Vance nodded. "Sure looks that way, sir."

"About your entry into the Square L," Captain Nelson continued. He opened a folder and slid out a paper. "Oh, yes. Here it is. It says here that you maintain you heard something inside the store and that's why you entered."

Vance's face colored. "Yes, sir."

"When you didn't have a warrant."

"Uh, that's right. Sir. I heard a call for help. That's when I investigated."

"Mm-hmm." When nothing else was forthcoming the captain looked over at Vance. "Don't stop now, detective. Where did you find Mr. Fadil? In what state was he?"

"I found him in Preston's office in the back of the store. He was bound and gagged."

The captain turned his attention back to

Ammar.

"You kill your brother, you turn him into a mummy, and then stash him in a corn field. May I ask why? What purpose did that serve?"

"I do believe I said go to hell," Ammar muttered. "And yes, you may quote me on that."

"It was his plan to cause pandemonium," Vance said, breaking the silence.

"It worked," one officer grumbled.

Several people snickered.

"How did you get the body into the corn field?" Vance asked. "There were people all over that corn maze, yet no one saw or heard a thing."

Ammar crossed his arms over his chest. His mouth became a thin line. Clearly, he was done talking.

Vance pulled the file they had on Victor Preston and skimmed through it. A look of triumph passed over his features. He handed the open folder to the captain.

"I believe I have the answer, sir."

The captain nodded. "Go ahead."

"Victor Preston may have been a convicted felon, but apparently he was firm believer in conservation."

"What does that mean?" I asked.

Vance tapped the report.

"Victor's car. It's electric. Do you have any idea how silent those things are? He simply drove his car into the corn field, dropped Ammar's brother off in the maze, and then left the same way he came. That's why no one heard anything."

"How did Ammar know which locker held the pendant?" I asked.

"You're looking at a lot of unfavorable crimes," Captain Nelson pointed out. "Unless you want me to get word to the Egyptian authorities about how uncooperative you've been, you will start cooperating. And yes, we've already notified the Egyptian Consulate. Your work visa has been revoked. You will be headed home, where I'm sure you'll be welcomed with open arms."

"Fine," Ammar muttered angrily. "If I'm going down, then I'm taking that idiot with me. Victor told me which locker held the pendant."

"How did Mr. Preston find out?" Captain Nelson asked.

"He overheard one of his employees talking on his cell during a break," Ammar slowly explained. "He got the kid drunk and plied him for information. Once we had the locker number, it was easy."

"How did you get the locker open without forcing it?" I asked.

Captain Nelson looked at me and I fell silent.

"Sorry," I mumbled. "I'll shut up now."

The captain waved a dismissive hand.

"Answer the question, Mr. Fadil. How did you get the locker open?"

"Please," Ammar scoffed. "Lockers for children with built-in combination locks? I could pick them with my eyes closed. It took me less than ten seconds to get in."

"Are you the one who stashed a bag of weed for us to find later?"

Ammar gave us a vindictive smile.

"It threw you off the scent, didn't it?"

"Not for long," Vance reminded him, which wiped the smile from his face.

"Looks like I owe Jimmy an apology," Captain Nelson muttered.

"He still stole the pendant and the mummy," Vance reminded him.

"True. So tell me something, Mr. Fadil."

Ammar's angry eyes looked into the captain's.

"Why haven't you left town? I would have thought that the instant the pendant was in your hands then you would've fled. Why didn't you?"

Ammar refused to answer.

"He was double-crossed," Vance guessed. "Looks like Victor couldn't pass up an opportunity to claim the pendant for himself. He got the drop on Ammar, tied him up, took the pendant, and left."

Ammar let his eyes drop to the ground and kept them there.

Captain Nelson motioned to several of the officers standing silently behind him. They nodded. One pulled Ammar to his feet and snapped a set of cuffs on his wrists.

"Ammar Fadil, you are being charged with the theft of property, possession of marijuana without a prescription, and contributing to the delinquency of a minor. I'm sure your country will be adding a charge of murder to that list once you're back."

He was led away as a dozen different conversations seemingly appeared out of nowhere. I heard the pendant and its present location get mentioned several times.

"That's enough, people," Captain Nelson said, as he addressed the group still in the room. "We will now focus all efforts on finding Mr. Preston. That will be all. Dismissed."

* * *

"You mean it? I don't have to go in tomorrow morning? Omigod, thank you so much, honey!"

Tori had wrapped her arms around her husband and was shaking with excitement. Vance gave her a spin before he set her down. He smiled at his wife.

"I told you that I'd get this figured out."

Tori blinked a few times at him. "Actually, you didn't."

Vance sighed. "Oh, just give me this moment, will you?"

"Oh, you big hunk of a stud, you. You are my knight in shining armor. Come with me now so I can show you how much I appreciate what you just did for me."

Vance's face turned Coke-can red.

"Tori! Knock it off! Not in front of our friends!"

Jillian and I both laughed. Vance and I had headed back to my house after Ammar had been officially charged. Jillian and Tori had been giggling like school girls, but instantly clammed up the moment we walked through the doors. From the looks on their faces, they must have been talking about one of us. Or both. It was hard to tell.

Sherlock and Watson were soon out cold. Sherlock was on his back on the couch, stretched out length-wise, with all four paws in the air. Watson was on the rug in front of the fireplace in her usual position, which I had found out from other corgi owners was often referred to as the 'Flying Squirrel': stretched out on the ground with both stumpy legs sticking directly out behind the dog, and the front two paws tucked close to the body but also facing backward. To me it looked horribly uncomfortable, but clearly, she must enjoy it.

"Did they recover the pendant?" Jillian hopefully asked.

"They will when they track down Victor Preston," Vance vowed. "He's got the pendant and he jumped ship. His store was abandoned, as was his house."

"Did Ammar confess to anything?" Tori wanted to know.

"He confessed to everything but killing his brother. I'm positive he killed his father, too. You should've seen the look on his face when I brought that up. Utter shock. I'm sure the Egyptian authorities will want to have a word with him."

Even though it was closing in on eleven

o'clock, the four of us were not ready to call it a night. We decided we wanted to celebrate. Tori called her friend, who was looking after her kids, and bribed her to stay a little longer.

Together we headed for the cars, intent on stopping by The Lonely Gringo, Pomme Valley's equivalent of a Denny's, for a bite to eat. Maybe a drink. They usually didn't close until midnight, so we had a little time. Plus, Vance tells me their terrace is open until midnight, too. It meant the dogs could come. I, on the other hand, had every intention of leaving them home. However, both dogs were instantly awake the moment both Jillian and I stood up. Somehow, and I still don't how they do it, they could tell we were planning on leaving.

"Just take them along," Vance said. "The owner is a buddy of mine. He loves dogs."

Sherlock and Watson ran for the door. Watson nudged one of the leashes. I looked at Tori and rolled my eyes.

"Does Anubis ever do this to you?" I asked.

"What, want to go on rides?" Tori asked. "Of course. They're dogs. They can tell when you're preparing to leave the house. They feel it is their job to protect you, so they want to come along. I already have a contingency plan in place if I ever want to leave the house without Anubis."

I watched Jillian collect her purse and put on her sweater.

"Oh, yeah? And what's that?"

"I have a spare pair of shoes in the garage, along

with a spare set of car keys. If I put on my shoes, or grab the keys off the holder while I'm still in the house, then Anubis knows."

I nodded. Spare shoes in the garage? Keys, too? That was actually a really good idea.

Five minutes later, with Jillian sitting in the passenger seat and both Sherlock and Watson in the back seat, I had just pulled my Jeep away from my driveway to follow Vance and Tori's sedan, when I saw their car come to a sudden stop. Unsure of what they were doing I pulled up alongside them. Thankfully, at this time of night there was no oncoming traffic. Jillian rolled her window down as she attempted to see if everything was okay.

"Vance is on the phone," Jillian quietly observed.

"How's he look?" I softly asked.

"Excited. Happy, even."

I propped myself up in my seat and tried to peer over Jillian's shoulder to see for myself.

"Really? That's gotta be good news, right?"

"He finished his call," Jillian informed me. "Now he's rolling his window down."

"Zack!" Vance's voice called out. "Jillian! You aren't gonna believe it!"

"What's the matter? I ... You ask him," I told Jillian. "You're closer."

"Is everything alright?" Jillian asked.

"They got him!" Vance excitedly told us. We each heard him whoop out loud.

"Fantastic!" I shouted back. "Meet you at the restaurant! We want to hear all about it!"

"He could have just called us," Jillian pointed out. "Between the four of us there are four cell phones involved."

Only when we were seated outside on the terrace at The Lonely Gringo, with our drinks in our hands and the dogs curled up at our feet, did we truly feel like the day was officially over. A quick glance across the street at the coffee shop's digital sign confirmed that this particular day only had about thirty more minutes left to it. I took a pull from my beer and sighed contentedly.

"So," I said as I addressed Vance, "where'd they get him?"

"The idiot was speeding in Portland. That's where they pulled him over. He's being transferred back here tomorrow."

"Did he have the necklace on him?" Tori hopefully asked, just before she took a sip of her drink.

"Pendant," Vance, Jillian, and I simultaneously corrected.

Tori almost snotted her margarita. She clapped a hand over mouth and hastily grabbed a napkin. Her eyes sparkled with amusement as she carefully swallowed her drink.

Vance nodded. "Yes. He had it stashed in a suitcase. They've taken pictures of it and have already sent them to the station. Dr. Tarik gave us strict instructions to notify him the instant the pendant was recovered. They've already let him know and wouldn't you know it? He's on his way to the station. He's currently studying the pictures we emailed him to be certain the pendant is undamaged. Apparently, his career is on the line and he would prefer to continue to be in the employ of Egyptian Exhibitions."

"Can't say that I blame him," I observed. "I'll bet he's relieved."

Together, we sat in silence as we watched several cars drive by on C Street.

"It's a beautiful night," Tori breathed, scooting her chair close to her husband's. She leaned up against him once he put an arm around her.

"It sure is. I'm so glad it's over."

Vance's cell shattered the moment.

"Oh, you gotta be kidding me," Vance grumbled as he pulled his cell out of his pocket. He looked at the caller ID and scowled. "Samuelson. Yeah, I'm awake. We're enjoying some quiet time at the ... what? Hold on. I'm putting you on speakerphone." Vance set his phone down on the table and tapped the screen. "Go ahead, Jones. Say that again."

I heard a man's voice begin to speak.

"I thought you should know, Detective. The pendant? The one they recovered from Victor Preston? It's a fake."

ELEVEN

T he following morning Vance and I were back at the station. This time I was standing with Captain Nelson on the other side of the one-way glass and watched as Vance entered the interrogation room and sat down on the same chair he had sat in when he had interrogated me. I know. I saw the familiar rips in the chair.

"How certain are you that the pendant is a fake?" I quietly asked the captain.

"A hundred percent."

"I don't get it. If Victor stole the fake pendant, then what happened to the real one?"

Captain Nelson turned to regard me.

"I thought you said you were a writer? Haven't you been able to figure this one out?"

"Why does everyone assume I'm a mystery writer?" I grumbled.

"Then what type of writer are you?" the captain asked.

"Can you just tell me what happened?"

"Victor Preston was double-crossed."

"By who?" I wanted to know.

Captain Nelson pointed at Ammar.

"Who else? Him."

"How can you be so certain?"

"I've been doing my job for more years than I care to count," Captain Nelson told me. "I pride myself for being able to read body language. I can tell almost immediately when someone is lying to me."

I had to order myself not to make a peep. He could pride himself? Please. I seem to recall the good captain maintained I was guilty when he thought I was the culprit behind the murders here a few months ago. It wasn't until the real killer made a full confession did he officially believe I was innocent.

However, at the moment he was acting cordial to me, so I really shouldn't push the issue.

"So what is Ammar's body language telling you now?"

"That he's hiding something."

"You think he knows that the pendant Victor absconded with is fake?"

"Of course. Look at his face. The guy is all but smirking. He thinks he's so smart. The fact is, the guy is as dumb as a bag of rocks."

I scratched the back of my head. "Come again?"

"Why else would he have stayed in town?" the captain asked me as he glanced my way. "He's stashed the pendant here in town. He thinks only he will be able to find it."

"Why isn't he worried?" I asked, bewildered.

"He's going to be sent away. He's not going to get a chance to recover the pendant. Why is he so smug?"

"Because he probably knows that his home country's penalties aren't nearly as severe as what they'd be here. Either he figures he can make it back here before it's found, or else he's going to send someone back here to claim it. Either way, that pendant needs to be found or else that smug sumbitch wins." The captain looked over at me and his face became grim. "Do you want that to happen? I sure don't. We need to find that pendant."

"He could have stashed it anywhere," I pointed out. "How in the world do you think we're going to be able to find it?"

We heard a commotion in the interrogation room. Vance was standing up and pushing his chair away from the table. He glanced once at us through the mirror and nodded his head toward the hallway. He wanted to talk to us out there.

I followed the captain out into the hallway and saw that they were huddled close together. Vance motioned me over.

"The captain says you two already figured out what I just gleaned from our uncooperative friend."

"The pendant is still in town," I guessed.

Vance nodded. "Right. We need to find it."

"How?" I asked.

Vance and the captain were both staring at me.

The clouds parted and a few rays of comprehension finally hit me. They were asking if Sherlock would take the case.

"Seriously? You think Sherlock can find it?"

"He found the tiger," Vance reminded me. "Let's see if he can find this pendant. Look, Zack. At this point it can't hurt to try. What do you say?"

"We can try. Just don't get your hopes up. Any idea where we should look?"

Vance shrugged. "I don't know. Maybe the school?"

I returned home to collect the dogs. Sherlock and Watson were absolutely thrilled with the prospect of going for another ride. I pushed open my front door and led both dogs out. I'm sure from the way they were both pulling that it must have looked like I was training the dogs to compete in the Iditarod. The only thing I needed in order to complete the picture was a sled.

Fifteen minutes later we were pulling up to the high school. Unfortunately, class was in session. But, I did get permission from Principal Reezen to wander the halls. He did make me promise that if the dogs found anything that I'd let him know personally. He also warned me I had about 30 minutes before the next bell sounded.

For half an hour we searched. The bell went off, turning the hallways into a maddening free-for-all as kids rushed to get to their next classes. I had quite a few of the students tell me how cute they thought the dogs were.

Ten minutes later, blissful silence. Lockers were slammed shut, classroom doors were closed, and my sanity returned. We explored the school grounds for close to an hour before we gave up. Sherlock simply had no interest in anything we looked at. Watson, on the other hand, was content to walk by my side as she watched her pack mate sniff at various items.

I called Vance and broke the bad news. I told him that the only thing I could do was possibly drive around town and see if Sherlock perked up at anything. He agreed. He told me that the Egyptian Embassy was sending two men to retrieve Ammar and should be there the following morning.

"I so want to rub this in his face," Vance told me. "Tell Sherlock that if he finds that pendant before Ammar is sent away, then I'll personally wear tights to our first dance lesson."

I laughed and hung up.

An hour later we broke for lunch. I placed a carryout order at Casa de Joe's, the town's only Mexican food restaurant, and surprised Jillian at work. Together we had lunch in her office.

"Have you guys had any luck yet?" Jillian asked after we disposed of the Styrofoam containers our lunch had come in.

"Nothing yet. I honestly don't know where to look. Ammar was MIA for close to two days. That's more than enough time to stash that pendant somewhere in town. Or out of town. Who knows?"

"So what are you going to do?" Jillian asked.

"I've got to keep looking. We need to find this pendant, Jillian."

Jillian laid a reassuring hand on mine.

"It's sweet of you to dedicate so much of your time to help Vance, but you have to consider that maybe we'll never find it. I know that would be a tremendous loss to the archaeological world, but it's just the way things happen."

I gave her hand a gentle squeeze.

"You don't understand. I have to find this thing."

"Why?" Jillian asked, puzzled.

"Because Vance said that he'd wear tights to his first dancing lesson if Sherlock finds the pendant."

Jillian's eyebrows shot straight up. A smile formed on her face. She pulled out her cell and sent off a text. Less than ten seconds later her phone chimed, signaling a message had been received. She read the message and burst out laughing.

"What?" I asked. I already figured she had texted Tori.

Jillian held her phone out to me. Yes, she had alerted Tori to what Vance had told me. Tori's response?

IF SHERLOCK FINDS THAT PENDANT THEN I'LL MAKE VANCE WEAR THE REST OF THAT COSTUME. PETER PAN. KEEP THIS BETWEEN US!

I snorted with laughter.

"We're heading back out. We've got ourselves a

missing pendant to locate."

Jillian was trying to hold back a case of the giggles.

"If you find it, please let me know, okay?"

I assured her she'd be the first to know if we did.

After two more hours of fruitless searching, I was forced to make another stop. Sherlock had started his performance of what I affectionately term his 'potty dance', which meant he had grown super fidgety and wouldn't stand still. We were nearing Gary's Grocery, which I knew had the large parking lot, and decided to stop there. Once Sherlock had completed his business, I was ready to head west, back into town, when I heard a woof.

I brought the Jeep to an immediate stop. I turned to look at Sherlock. He, in turn, was staring out the window, straight at ... the Square L. He woofed again. Curious, I turned right instead of left and drove toward the darkened store. Sherlock's barks became more persistent.

My hopes soared. Could Ammar have hidden the real pendant right under Victor Preston's nose? I parked, let the dogs out, and walked toward the store. Watson was uninterested with the store, but Sherlock continued to bark. He led me straight to the back door and pawed at it with one of his stumpy legs.

I pulled out my cell and called Vance.

"Zack? What's up? Do you need ... wait. Wait! Did you find it??"

"We're back at the Square L," I told Vance.

"I've driven all over this town and Sherlock hasn't given me even the softest of growls. However, I drove by the store and he started to lose his mind. He took me straight back to the back door."

"The same one from last night?"

"Yep. Unless you've got the keys to this place, then I'm not gonna be able to do much here."

"Stay right there. I'm on my way."

Fifteen minutes later Vance was there. He pulled out a silver key ring with three different keys on it. He unlocked the door on the second attempt.

"How'd you get keys to this place?" I asked.

"Preston's night manager turned in her set, right after she officially resigned. I didn't know what else to do with them so I kept them locked in my desk."

Vance pushed open the door and switched on the lights. Sherlock pushed his way past the detective and took the lead. I tapped Vance on the shoulder to get his attention.

"Should I drop the leash? There's nothing in this store that can hurt him, is there?"

Vance shook his head. "No. It's perfectly safe. Go ahead."

I dropped the leash. Sherlock turned to look up at me with a look of amazement on his canine features. I nodded.

"You wanted to check this place out, pal. Well, here we are. Let's see if our friend here is gonna have to wear tights to his first dance class."

"Oops. I forgot about that."

"Rest assured that I haven't, buddy."

"If he finds it, you'd better not hold me to it," Vance warned.

"If he finds it then you'd better pick out a pair of tap shoes," I returned.

"Whatever. There's no way Tori would let me out of the house in that getup."

I had to bite my tongue. If you only knew, dude. That was going to be the Kodak moment of the century.

Sherlock turned to head into the main part of the store. He wove his way through the aisles of snacks, jerky, and candy bars and stopped at the chips section. The little corgi promptly sat, turned to look up at me, and gave one of his low howls.

"Awwooooo!"

I looked over at Vance. My detective friend looked worried. I would be, too, if I had been dumb enough to agree to put on tights. In public.

"What do you have?" I asked, as I joined Vance at the rack of potato chips and corn chips. "See anything?"

Vance started pulling bags off the shelf. Nothing. Nothing was hiding behind the products nor did it look like any of the bags had been tampered with.

"Are you sure he wants us to look over here?" Vance asked, turning to look down at Sherlock.

"He hasn't moved," I pointed out. "Whatever

he wants us to find has gotta be right here."

Vance and I began emptying shelf after shelf of bags of snacks. Several dozen bags of potato chips, pork rinds, and corn chips fell unceremoniously to the floor. It wasn't until we made it to the bottom shelf, where the tubes of snacks were, that Sherlock started to bounce up and down on his front legs, as though I was bouncing a ball and he was eager for me to throw it.

"I think we're getting closer," I mused, sweeping tubes of Pringles onto the ground.

"Please don't be here, please don't be here, please don't be here," Vance softly chanted.

I laughed and continued to search. I had just swept the last of the tubes onto the ground when I paused. I had heard a metallic clunk. Granted, these types of snacks weren't the best for you, and they were probably going to end up resembling a lump in your gut, but they still shouldn't sound like that when knocked to the floor.

I began picking up the last batch of tubes I had knocked over. One of the tubes, a red original-flavored tube of Pringles, felt heavier than the rest. And it jingled when I gently shook the tube.

"What do you have there?" Vance asked, alarmed.

I looked up and grinned. I do believe the good detective was looking a wee bit pale. I popped open the top of the tube and saw that the safety seal was still in place but it had been peeled almost off. I peeled back the seal and looked inside the tube. There were no chips inside. I tipped the tube over and felt something heavy plop into my hand.

It was the infamous, priceless, Nekhbet Pendant, once worn by King Tut himself. I turned to Vance and held up the ugly piece of vulture-shaped jewelry to my friend and grinned at him. Vance groaned.

"First pair is on me. Do you prefer control top or would you like fishnet?"

EPILOGUE

W ould you stop laughing? What kind of dog owner ridicules their own dogs?"

I wiped the tears from my eyes.

"What kind of dog owner dresses up their dogs in silly getups like that?" I countered.

Jillian and I were strolling arm in arm along the rows of vendors set up behind the main storefront at Greentree Gardens. At the moment, Jillian was holding both leashes while I carried a number of bags. It felt as though we had purchased something from every single tent we had passed.

Sherlock and Watson, typically found in front of our procession whenever we went on our walks, trailed behind us on this particular day. Looking miserable. If ever a dog could throw a human a dirty look, it'd be Sherlock. Since Halloween seemed to be celebrated the entire month of October in PV, and since I've seen quite a few people also dressed in costumes, I had suggested that perhaps we should get costumes.

Not for me. Don't be silly. For the dogs.

Jillian had thought it was a delightful idea. She

had instantly found several websites that catered to canine costumes. She picked out a couple she thought were adorable, I paid for them, and I got to watch Jillian put them on the dogs.

Sherlock was dressed up as … Sherlock Holmes. He was wearing a small deerstalker hat, complete with a strap that went under his chin—he tried every ten seconds or so to dislodge the irksome accessory—and a tweed cape that stretched down his elongated torso almost to his hind end. Like the hat, it too had elastic straps to keep the costume in place.

Watson was wearing a Coachman's style bowler hat, a brown tweed 'jacket' that encompassed the majority of her torso, and had a tiny cane attached to the left side of her jacket. She, too, had tried to dislodge the cumbersome attire that we had dressed her in, but at least she only tried every minute or so as opposed to Sherlock's incessant shaking. Watson kept throwing me traitorous looks, as though she believed I no longer loved her.

"You really need to stop laughing," Jillian whispered, looking apologetically down at the dogs. "They're making me feel bad for suggesting we buy them costumes."

"Oh, they're fine. I thought it was a clever idea, dressing them as their namesakes."

Vance and Tori appeared, leading Anubis on a leash. The elegant German Shepherd, also outfitted in a costume, looked none too happy with his owners, either. Anubis was also dressed as his namesake, complete with headdress, golden chest plate, and an intricate golden blanket running down his back.

Everyone oohed and aahed over the dogs. We laughed, we joked, and we had a good time. Walking alongside Jillian, with her hand in mine, felt good--natural. I had believed for far too long that I would never be happy again after my beloved Samantha died. I had thought that my life was over, that I had nothing to live for. Looking down at the two dogs reluctantly following behind us, and then over at Jillian, who smiled every time she looked my way, I began to feel normal again. I was surprised to realize that I had started looking forward to waking up every morning.

Here, in this small rinky-dink town of Pomme Valley, I truly felt like I was home.

AUTHOR'S NOTE

My plan for this novel was to have it released by Halloween. I thought having a subject with the words "Fleet-Footed Mummy" in the title would be cool and very appropriate to the time of year. But, life finds a way to derail the train, no matter how stable/sturdy the tracks appear to be. So I didn't quite make it.

But, I had a lot of fun revisiting Zack and the corgis in scenic Pomme Valley. This time they were visited by a traveling Egyptian side show and, naturally, nothing goes as planned. However, now that order has been restored, the question becomes, what now? Well, life will return to normal, but only for about a month (Pomme Valley time).

Case of the Holiday Hijinks is due to be released a few days before Christmas. Zack and the corgis are called in to see if they can figure out how presents keep disappearing from under the tree, all without any signs of forced entry. Money doesn't appear to be a factor, so what is the motivation for stealing the presents?

By now I'm sure you're thinking, in time for Christmas? Isn't Christmas less than two months away? Yes. Yes it is. Time to get crackin'! Happy reading!

J.
November, 2016

Zack and the corgis will be back in time for Christmas in *Case of the Holiday Hijinks*!

There's a Grinch in Pomme Valley! Someone is stealing presents right from under the noses of unsuspecting home owners and leaving no trace of how he broke in. Corgis Sherlock and Watson are on the case! The townsfolk are scared. City officials are nervous. Can Zack and the dogs put a stop to this crime spree before Christmas is ruined for everyone?

Sign up for Jeffrey's newsletter on his website to get all the latest corgi: www.AuthorJMPoole.com

The Corgi Case Files Series
Available in e-book and paperback

Have you missed any in the series?

Case of the One-Eyed Tiger
Case of the Fleet-Footed Mummy
Case of the Holiday Hijinks
Case of the Pilfered Pooches
Case of the Muffin Murders
Case of the Chatty Roadrunner
Case of the Highland House Haunting
Case of the Ostentatious Otters
Case of the Dysfunctional Daredevils
Case of the Abandoned Bones
Case of the Great Cranberry Caper

If you enjoy Epic Fantasy, check out Jeff's other series:
Pirates of Perz
Tales of Lentari
Bakkian Chronicles

Made in United States
Orlando, FL
28 December 2021

12618362R00162